SCRIVENER'S HEART

Chloe Taton

For Zeke, whose conversation inadvertently inspired the premise for this book.

Chapter 1

The alarm clock flicked over to 8:00 AM and began beeping, signaling the arrival of another weekday morning. Latisha Robbins rolled out of bed with a muffled groan and crossed the room to silence the alarm. She'd learned long ago that if she kept her alarm clock within reach of the bed, she'd fall back asleep as soon as she shut it off. Walking was the only way to make sure her brain got the message.

She glanced at her phone, confirming that it was, in fact, Friday. Good. Only 5,000 words of drafting stood between her and the weekend, two whole days and an evening where she wouldn't have to think about intricate pseudo-Victorian fashion, clockwork, swashbuckling gentleman burglars, or romance in general. And she was right at the beginning of a draft, before her loathing for what she was doing could build up too much, meaning she'd be able to push through those 5,000 words relatively quickly.

There had been a time when Latisha had felt vaguely guilty for how much she disliked working as a writer. Becoming an author had been her deepest desire for years, and was something that would be a dream come true for countless struggling writers out there. But then, the writing wasn't the problem.

The problem was what she had to write about.

Yawning and managing to avoid stumbling into her dresser for once, she made the bed, showered, dressed, and considered styling her hair. Moments later, she wrangled her curls into a messy bun behind her head, promising, as always, to deal with the tangles later. A breakfast of toast and coffee nudged her over the line into full awareness. She contemplated going for a walk around the block to reinforce the notion, but decided against it, recognizing it for the procrastination it was.

Come on, Latisha. You're stronger than Rodrigo Antúnez and this stupid book. Get going. The sooner you start, the sooner you'll be done for the day.

With a sigh, she took herself to the apartment's small guest room turned office, where her PC sat slumbering innocently on her desk. Above the monitor, on a small shelf built into the desk, stood a row of paperbacks, with spines that seemed to radiate luridness despite being various shades of brown, bronze, and gold. The most recent addition, closest to the end, featured a tanned, muscular man with flowing dark hair perched in the crosstrees of what looked like a flying clipper ship on its cover. The man wore a half-open, lacy white shirt, tight pants, and an impressive number of gear-covered pistols. The cover bore elaborate raised lettering announcing the title as *Robbery Under Charm*, while smaller lettering detailed that it had been written by Amora Ellis and that it was twelfth in the Rakish Heart series.

The Amora Ellis identity had been Latisha's main stipulation when she first started writing the foul things, fresh out of college. At the time, she'd still held out hope that someday she'd be able to write something real, something serious and thoughtful and laden with deeper meaning. She might have had to waste her first good idea on this pile of tawdry romantic drivel to pay the bills, but surely, eventually, she'd get the chance to write things she'd actually want her real name associated with.

At least, that was what she'd always thought.

But that was several years ago now, and Latisha was beginning to think she should've just her own name from the start. She had money now from royalties, but the publishing house kept pushing for more of Rodrigo's adventures—and who could blame them?

The books sold like hotcakes.

But it meant she never had time anymore to write things she really wanted to write. After forcing herself to write lurid treacle five days every week, Latisha just couldn't find it in her to type even one more word.

She sat, powered on the computer, and opened up where she'd last saved the document. What had been going on? Oh yes, Rodrigo had just manufactured an encounter with the latest in a string of rich, beautiful young women whose hearts he would capture and toss aside and whose heirloom jewelry he would steal.

His current target was called Lady Jennifer Bartram. So far, Latisha had determined that she had red hair (*"flowing auburn tresses that brushed her porcelain throat"*) and was the owner of a fabulous necklace featuring an emerald known as the Star of Atlantis (*"The stone was the deep green of a sylvan pool, but even clearer and more fathomless"* — or would that work better for her eyes?), which had been in her family three generations.

"My lady," Rodrigo said smoothly, pressing his lips to the cool, soft knuckles of her white hand, "I shall count the hours until we meet again."

"And I shall do the same," Lady Jennifer replied, her green eyes flashing in amusement and interest. "It is not every day one encounters a man so swift-tongued and prepossessing, so quick of wit and action, and so much of a gentleman as you yourself are."

Latisha rolled her eyes and leaned back in her chair.

Rodrigo was a scapegrace and an incorrigible flirt, a reckless thief who used his pretty face and appeal to get ahead just because he could, regardless of how many broken hearts he stepped on or how often he put his crew in danger. Latisha hated him. She hated the terrible stereotypes he embodied. She hated having to write characters who fell for him anyway.

And she hated that she had made him what he was.

Several hours plus a break for lunch later, she let her head fall to the desk with a slight thud. It was done. She'd hit her word count, meaning she didn't have to think about Rodrigo and his gang of scalawags for a whole weekend.

Desperately in need of a stretch, Latisha dragged her head up and tried to shove her desk chair back to stand up. One of the wheels of the chair caught on the edge of the rug, and her seat tilted out from underneath her. She fell, bracing herself to hit the floor—

And instead found herself wincing in pain when she collided with stone. Shaken, Latisha raised her head and looked around. She seemed to be lying in a cobblestone-paved alleyway, next to an old-fashioned brick wall. Everything seemed a little more . . . saturated, particularly the brown tones, and it smelled peculiar, like smoke, metal, and oil, and lots of people who had all packed in together and were trying to compensate for it.

I must've hit my head harder than I thought, Latisha mused with remarkable calm. She'd fallen so hard she'd given herself a concussion, and ended up at the hospital somehow, and they'd dosed her with something really good, because how else had she found herself outdoors, staring out of an alleyway at people in distinctly steampunk clothing?

Her gaze darted around, alighting on designs and features she knew better than the backs of her hands—clock faces scattered over the buildings, including some truly impractical spots; carriages being pulled along by gleaming mechanical quadrupeds; extravagant, crowded architecture that combined brick, glass, and ornately twisted metal.

It had to be a dream or a hallucination, brought on by stress over the deadline on *Pride and Persuasion*, because the Rakish Heart world was fictional. It didn't exist, thank goodness.

There was no way she was physically present in it.

Latisha did her best to get to her feet—her bare feet, she realized. For some reason, her imagination had left her dressed as she had been at home, in jeans and a comfortable magenta blouse and no footwear at all. Pulling herself up against the nearby brick wall stung her abused palms enough to suggest that maybe this was real, but she shoved the ridiculous notion aside.

It was more likely that she'd finally started to crack under the stress of constantly waxing poetic about settings like this, and her brain had created a lifelike representation of her fictional world to help her be more descriptive going forward. In that case, she supposed she might as well look around and take mental notes in case she could use any of this later.

Latisha took a few experimental steps, found she could walk normally, and edged her way into the flow of people passing in the street. They were all fairly well-dressed from what she remembered of her invented social structures, meaning they were probably upper-middle-class. The area seemed to mostly consist of row houses, while the crowd seemed to mostly consist of women's bustles and men's canes that were evidently intent on making her dodge and squeeze through them to get anywhere at all.

It didn't help that she was attracting a lot of odd looks — probably not because of her darker skin tone, given that the people around her represented a wide variety of racial backgrounds, but likely because of her clothes.

Latisha had cultivated a wardrobe free of lace, embroidery, and anything brown since the first Amora Ellis book was published, which had seemed like a sound decision at the time, but was something she was now regretting. She was uncomfortably aware that her blouse was a non-native hue that not even the most hapless alchemist in her world could hope to replicate.

Not that she was in the *Raking Heart* world. Of course not.

Scanning through the crowd for an available path forward, her eyes landed on a small but familiar figure. A petite teenage Black girl, in a slightly-too-short white dress and overlarge leather boots, was moving against the flow of pedestrians with a distinctive creeping, furtive gait. She seemed to go unnoticed by the adults surrounding her, which was just as well, because she was clearly picking their pockets and depositing the contents into the recesses of her pocket-laden green vest.

Latisha knew that girl. She knew her quite well. She was Ruby, cabin girl of the *Rake*, part of Rodrigo Antúnez' crew. But she was supposed to be on the ship, cleaning or something—the crew usually tried to keep her away from actual crime, didn't they? And even if they didn't, since when did Rodrigo's carefree band have to resort to something as unglamorous as petty theft?

This was becoming a bridge too far even for a dream. Latisha had never so much as imagined anything like that for the crew.

She started pushing her way through more determinedly, never taking her eyes off her fast-moving character. She was still far from sold on this being in any way real, but her curiosity was getting the better of her, and she wanted answers even if they were hallucinatory ones.

Unfortunately, while she was still a good few yards and an eternity of shoving away from her target, Ruby looked up and met her eyes. The girl took off, abandoning all traces of furtiveness, and bolted for a nearby alleyway. Being smaller, she was able to get through faster, weaving through obstacles that would have blocked a full-size adult.

Latisha let out a huff of breath and commenced fighting her way through the crowd more firmly than before. She wasn't going to give up that easily, and she wasn't about to let a character she'd invented herself give her the slip.

. . . Assuming this was real, of course.

The words were sounding weaker and weaker every moment.

Chapter 2

Rodrigo checked his reflection one last time in the shop window he was waiting near. Clothes clean and neat, but not too formal, suit jacket buttoned strategically to conceal where his leather waistcoat had been patched with crimson silk, hair loose and most weapons hidden so as to not immediately give away that he was a skydweller. He was as ready as he would ever be to confront his target.

This wouldn't be the first time he'd met her—he'd manufactured an encounter about a week and a half ago, in which he'd finagled his way into a soiree she was attending and chatted with her for twenty minutes or so. It was a toss-up whether she would remember him or not, but he rather thought she would. Lady Jennifer had seemed possessed of a sharper mind than the usual run of society women he made a living off of. That would likely make his job more challenging, but he wasn't about to complain. Challenge, a little extra bit of danger, and the ensuing adrenaline rush were what made the heists fun.

He could hear the distinct sounds of a carriage approaching— that would be Lady Jennifer now. It was lucky for him that she was wealthy enough to keep her own horse-powered transportation; clock-carriages were a good deal more difficult to sabotage. With horses, all you had to do was learn the target's routes and watch for a steep downhill, get the driver a little tipsy at the right moment, lie in wait and startle the animals, and run like mad once the carriage took off at a sufficiently alarming speed.

Well, Lady Jennifer's driver *had* proved incorruptible on the alcohol front, but that wasn't a completely vital part of the plan, anyway. The pair of horses pulling Lady Jennifer's conveyance panicked right on cue when the street boy Rodrigo had bribed sent a tiny, scrappy, angrily yapping dog right into their path. They reared up, nearly upsetting the carriage, then took off down the street. Rodrigo grinned and sprinted after them. The driver was trying hard enough to get them under control and Rodrigo was skilled enough at dodging pedestrians that he was able to catch up without too much trouble, just as the vehicle was about to careen down a particularly steep hill.

That . . . wasn't optimal.

He'd intended to get hold of the horses' heads just before they reached the incline, so he could stage a narrow escape for Lady Jennifer and her driver. At this point, though, he wouldn't be able to slow them down enough before the carriage picked up enough momentum to run into the animals, wrecking the vehicle and injuring everyone involved. Time for Plan B, then. He'd pulled off this version once before.

As the carriage went over the crest of the hill, he took a running leap and caught hold of the door handle, pulling himself up onto the running board. The driver felt the weight shift and looked back as if to give him a piece of his mind, but Rodrigo ignored him, focusing on getting the door open without knocking himself off. By some process of acrobatics he wasn't sure he'd be able to duplicate, he finally managed it, swinging his way into the carriage and coming face-to-face with a very startled Lady Jennifer.

"My lady," he greeted, offering a charming smile and something like a bow. "You look as though you could use some assistance."

He didn't give her time to respond, looping an arm around her waist and pulling her close against him, then leaping out of the still-open carriage door. The heavy skirts of her extravagantly ornamented dark green dress made it a little more difficult to get her to move the way he needed her to, but he was able to twist them both so he hit the ground first, with her ending up sprawled on top of him. Absently, some part of his brain noticed that her perfume smelled of lilies, and her fashionably loose hair had contrived to fall so it framed her collarbone a little too perfectly. He wondered if ladies' maids deliberately set out to achieve such an effect in these situations—it couldn't be coincidental.

A short ways off, he could hear the multi-part crash as the carriage hit, followed by the loud whinny of disgruntled horses. He hoped the driver had gotten clear.

He hadn't the faintest idea what to say next, but wasn't terribly worried. These things tended to take care of themselves, he'd found.

"Señor del Rey," Lady Jennifer said, slightly breathlessly, addressing him by the false name he'd given before. "It seems you have a knack for impeccable timing."

Ah, and here it came, the words falling off of his tongue without him deciding to say them—unnerving, yes, but useful for the moment. "I can take no credit for it, my lady," he said easily, maneuvering himself to his feet and setting her upright in one smooth motion. "It must have been pure good fortune that brought me to your aid in your time of need."

Lady Jennifer was only a couple of inches shorter than him in the heels she was wearing, but she still managed to look up at him through her eyelashes. "Perhaps it was nothing more nor less than fate."

"A reasonable enough conclusion. The Fates could not possibly abide letting such a lovely lady meet an untimely end through such an accident."

In truth, Rodrigo was pretty sure he didn't believe in fate, either as an abstract concept or as one or more personifications. He didn't even believe in it enough to joke about it being real. There was just you, the situation at hand, the resources available, your own wits, and the occasional odd turn of luck to get you through the day.

So he wasn't entirely sure where these words were coming from —they definitely weren't anything he would normally say. But then, he reasoned, a lot of the things he said to his marks didn't make much sense, so this wasn't that unusual.

Several minutes of hopefully productive conversation later—it wasn't like he needed to pay much attention when the words always seemed to suit the situation—he managed to extricate himself from Lady Jennifer. He made a show of paying her fare in a passing clock-carriage for hire and started on his way home.

A quick glance at his pocket watch confirmed that he was definitely late to rendezvous with the *Rake*. He could only hope the rope ladder was still waiting, and they hadn't been forced to move on. Law enforcement might not be able to catch them in the air but staying low for too long with a clear path up from street level was asking for trouble.

Linn would most definitely be irritated with him for keeping them all waiting.

He could move faster and see better from the rooftops, and it was the work of a moment to scale a nearby drainpipe and ascend to the peak of the nearest building. There were a fair few ships visible in the clouded, smoky sky. Most of them legitimately owned gasbags, but there were a few sails from skyships drifting here and there. He slipped a spyglass from an inside pocket of his coat and after a minute or two of scanning the horizon, found what he was looking for several streets away—the *Rake*'s familiar figurehead depicting a robed maiden with a clockwork right arm. Moreover, he could make out two small figures—probably Asad and Linn, the navigator and the first mate—hauling the rope ladder up over the side.

He had, as suspected, missed his window, not that that would necessarily stop him.

Rodrigo took note of the direction, stowed the spyglass away, and took off running lightly along the rooftops, leaping from one to the next easily. The buildings in this part of town were close enough together that he barely had to jump at all, and he only had to shimmy down, cross at ground level, and clamber back up to the roofs at a few intersections.

The *Rake* had started to move, slowly but surely, by the time he got close, and the rope ladder had been completely hauled in. They hadn't gained any altitude yet, though, so either Linn was stalling or Asad hadn't had time to take them back to a safe height.

With a quick glance at his surroundings, Rodrigo waited, then scrambled up a particularly high chimney just as the *Rake* passed by. In the nick of time, he leapt, caught the bowsprit, swung himself onto it and slid down onto the deck.

He only had a moment to enjoy the success before he spotted Linn coming towards him, a dark look on her face. He spread his arms apologetically. "Sorry I didn't make the rendezvous. Lady Jennifer's carriage was running late—"

"We've got a bigger problem to deal with," Linn interrupted, and he realized the look on her face wasn't actually meant for him. "We took advantage of the ladder being down to send Ruby on an errand, and somebody followed her back to the ship."

Chapter 3

Latisha was far past ready to wake up.

Her feet were sore and abraded from chasing Ruby over cobblestone streets without shoes, and her arms and shoulders were aching from the death grip on the rope ladder that she'd only just relinquished.

The impulsive decision to follow Ruby even when she left the ground had made perfect sense at the time, but the ascent had taken long enough that she'd had far too much time to think that she'd made a mistake.

I've never had a dream that hurt this much before. What if I'm not hallucinating and I'm actually in danger here?

Similar thoughts rattled through her brain, even as the air temperature dropped rapidly as she was pulled higher, and as she sprawled onto the solidness of the deck with a thump. The smoky smell of the caulking between the planks registered as her nose pressed into the wood.

There were people standing over her, and she knew them as she'd known Ruby. Closest to her was Linn Hafidi, first mate of the *Rake* and Rodrigo's right hand, immediately recognizable by her habitual long fawn-colored coat, the braid of dark-brown hair down her back, and a glare that wasn't to be trifled with. The tanned, stocky, bearded man to her right was Linn's husband Asad—even if Latisha hadn't known him by his engineer's apron and navigator's goggles, she would have guessed from the faint ticking that hinted at him being an automaton.

Latisha remembered characterizing them as reasonable individuals who nonetheless bought into Rodrigo's unlikely schemes. She hoped that was true, because she was starting to get the horrifying suspicion that that this *wasn't* a dream or hallucination.

She really was in the world of the *Rakish Heart* series, meaning that she needed to provide an explanation to Linn and Asad before they did something extreme, like throwing her overboard. They were decent people, but they had limits, and she'd rather not test those limits if she could help it.

Linn's glare deepened. "You've got about a minute to explain why you thought it was a good idea to hitch a ride on our ship. Who are you and what do you want with our cabin girl?"

"My name's La—Amora," Latisha started, only to find her mouth changing the words without her brain's permission. She swallowed a few times, then tried to push past the strange block. "I mean, it's La—Lat—Amora. Amora Ellis."

Her chest started to knot up with fear. Why couldn't she say her real name? Why was she only able to utter her terrible, tacky pseudonym?

She shuddered for a moment, then let out a long sigh. "Fine. My name's Amora. That girl—the one I followed—she stole from me, all the money I had—I have to get it back."

Both of them still looked more skeptical than anything else.

The thought panicked her enough that, in desperation, she resorted to the oldest cliche in the book—a fainting fit—to buy more time.

She kept her eyes cracked open just a little, though, to try and take in everything around her. She'd assumed the ship picking Ruby up would be the *Rake*, and the sight of the figurehead confirmed it. But what she was looking at now wasn't just the *Rake* of her romances—long on flowery language and short on technical specifics.

15

This was the *Rake* as she hadn't pictured it since her idealistic early days as a writer, when she'd dreamed of writing real steampunk and had done ridiculous amounts of research on clipper ships to make everything as accurate as possible. This *Rake* was a working vessel, insofar as that could be true of a sailing ship that flew at high altitudes by means she'd never gotten the chance to fully flesh out.

Linn's voice interrupted her thoughts. "Ruby, come over here, please."

Light footsteps indicated that the girl had drawn closer.

"She says you stole from her," Linn said, softly and calmly. "Did you take anything from her, that would be valuable enough for her to chase you all this way? I thought you were sticking to the better-off areas of town."

Ruby shook her head. "I didn't even go near her. I wouldn't pickpocket somebody like that—I wouldn't even know how, with those clothes. I saw her, of course; she'd have been hard to miss. But I didn't think much of her until she started following me."

"So who did rob her, then? Any other pickpocket would've probably avoided her for the same reasons you did—difficult to manage and looks broke anyway," Asad pointed out. "Not to mention that it's rare to find two pickpockets in the same street in that part of the city."

"There wasn't anyone else working that area, not that I saw," Ruby confirmed. "I don't know how she got robbed; all I know is that it wasn't me."

A thump by the hatch announced that Grammy, the ship's cook and final crew member, had joined them on deck. Latisha couldn't see her, but she heard her gruff voice asking, "What's all the fuss about?"

Asad briefly recounted the events of the past few minutes. "She doesn't seem to be a threat, so we can't kill her," he concluded, "but we can't just drop her off somewhere either. Oh, and Rodrigo's half an hour late getting back from trying to worm his way into Lady Jennifer's good graces."

Well, that answered a couple of Latisha's questions in a mostly reassuring fashion.

Grammy harrumphed. "Bring her below. I'll see if I can find something sharp-smelling in the galley to bring her 'round. You better make up your mind what you think of her before the captain gets back, or he'll decide she's a hapless waif and make her part of the crew."

That was less reassuring. Latisha didn't want to see Rodrigo, let alone have to share living space with him. Then again, if she couldn't find a way to make . . . whatever this was stop, where else could she go?

Someone gathered her up off the deck and carried her below. What little she could see confirmed that all where it should be— the galley, the mess area that doubled as a general gathering spot, and the weapons cupboard were all exactly where she'd placed them. She guessed purely from location that the cabin she was being carried into was Grammy and Ruby's, and despite everything, felt a tiny bit gratified when the presence of a half-knitted shawl on the chair and a dime novel on the top bunk confirmed her speculation.

Latisha was distracted enough by this that it took her a moment after being settled on the lower bunk (Grammy's) to realize that the word "captain" kept coming up in the others' muttered conversation.

She jerked back into near-panic immediately. There hadn't been enough time for her to plan yet. If she had to meet Rodrigo, she'd probably either start screaming, burst out laughing, or slap him across the face, none of which would be helpful in this situation. Whatever "this situation" actually was.

Grammy's voice cut through her thoughts. "Ruby, fetch me the gunpowder garlic."

Gunpowder garlic? What's that?

Latisha had just enough time to wonder what that gap in her

knowledge might mean before Ruby's light footsteps returned and someone sat down on the edge of the thin mattress.

The most pungent, malodorous substance known to man was then shoved into Latisha's face. It smelled akin to garlic and hot peppers, but mostly like pain and long-fermented gym socks.

Latisha jerked and twisted away, sneezing several times and thoroughly ruining her ruse of unconsciousness in the process. Quite possibly, that was the point.

The primary thought in her head, though, more than disgust or worrying about appearances and interrogations, was the realization that *I can't be hallucinating, I couldn't possibly imagine anything that horrible. How is this happening? What do I do?*

Reeling, she managed to look around and spotted Grammy, white-haired and bony and wearing a worn gray dress and apron, regarding her with satisfaction from her seat on the end of the bunk as she closed up the jar of a yellowish powder that had to be gunpowder garlic.

Latisha gathered her sprawled legs to herself somewhat and scooted as far away as possible. "What was that for?"

"Works better than smelling salts," Grammy said a touch proudly. "Don't blame you for fainting after that trip up the ladder —I never use it if I can help it—but we had to wake you up so you could explain your situation to the captain."

No. No. No, no, no. She should have predicted this and run far in the other direction while she still could. "Now?" Latisha managed, hating how small her voice sounded. She was not going to turn into one of her own brainless, spineless leading ladies.

"Only if you're up to it . . . Amora, did you say your name was?" came another voice from the cabin doorway. Latisha looked, already knowing who she was going to see. There was only one person, in the Rakish Heart world or any other, who had a voice like that—smooth as silk and rich as expensive chocolate.

Rodrigo Antúnez was leaning against the door frame, arms crossed and watching her with an intense focus.

She could practically hear her internal narrator describing him—*ostensibly relaxed, but with a latent tension in his lean, muscled frame. The light from a flickering lantern gleamed on his tanned skin and on the flowing raven hair escaping from its short tail, and reflected in his dark, fiery eyes—*

But there she made herself stop, because in several little ways he *wasn't* like she'd expected. She had always imagined him with a perpetual cocky, charming smile, instead of the more thoughtful expression he now wore. He was showing a little more wear than she would have guessed, too—there were faint lines around his eyes and mouth that she wouldn't have expected from a man in his early thirties, his waistcoat had a large patch in it, and his clothes were rather scuffed and dusty.

Of course. She'd just been writing the carriage rescue scene with Lady Jennifer. He'd probably just come back from that.

The thought brought on a rush of mental images of all the stories she'd ever written about him, especially the scenes where he would seduce women and the scenes where he would leave them flat.

The reminder was enough to promptly squash any thrills she might otherwise have felt when meeting her protagonist in the flesh.

Latisha still didn't want to believe this was all real, but until she could prove it wasn't, she had probably better act as if it was. That was better getting herself killed by being stupid and foolhardy.

And that meant dealing with Rodrigo.

Chapter 4

Rodrigo watched the woman who'd intruded on his ship, waiting to see what she would do.

Linn hadn't exaggerated when she said the newcomer was strange—he'd never seen clothes like that before, and his criminal career had brought him into contact with all manner of strange fashion choices. Her curly black hair was pulled into a messy bun at the nape of her neck, which suggested she was a skydweller. No one living up here for long would be stupid enough to keep long hair loose, where the wind could snatch it and tangle it beyond all hope of fixing with a comb, and down below, it was fashionable to style hair loosely to distinguish oneself from the criminal class.

If she *was* a skydweller, it was possible that she'd been trying to get to her own ship and gotten the wrong ladder . . . but in that case she would have said so, instead of babbling nonsense and fainting.

It was also possible that she was pretending to be disturbed to put them off guard in order to attack them all later, but if she were trying the helpless waif act, she'd have been better served to leave her hair down like she'd never been in the air before.

The faint had probably been faked, though. She currently looked a little shaky and wild-eyed, but not nearly enough to have actually passed out.

He raised an eyebrow. "So. That explanation?" he asked.

For some reason, she startled when he spoke again, but after a moment, she seemed to find some resolve and straightened her spine. "Yes. I'm . . . Amora Ellis. I assume you're the captain of this ship?"

Rodrigo nodded, filing away the hesitance over her name for future reference. Linn had mentioned there'd been some oddities about that, as well. "Rodrigo Antúnez, at your service." He gave a slight head-bow—just enough of one to not break his line of sight, not until he knew more about her and what she wanted. "Everyone, I think perhaps this conversation should be conducted more privately. I will call if any of you are needed—Ruby, that includes you on both counts."

He'd thought perhaps Ruby would be reluctant to leave, but she was the first out the door, barely giving him enough time to move from the frame. Clearly, she didn't want to stay in sight of the mysterious Miss Ellis any longer than necessary.

Linn and Asad followed in due order. Grammy was the last out, giving him a sharp look as she went. He winked—the action impossible for Amora to see from where she was—confirming that he'd be fine on his own.

For such a gruff woman, Grammy could be a worrywart in the oddest ways.

As his crew finished filing out, he turned back to examining the newcomer. Amora, to his surprise, looked like she was being left alone with a sewer rat, or something else both disgusting and dangerous.

Rodrigo briefly wondered what he'd done to earn that kind of trepidation from someone who allegedly didn't even know him, but then refocused on the task at hand. He needed to get to the bottom of this. Ruby wasn't supposed to go around stealing from people—as far as he was aware, she'd never committed a crime in her life. Not to mention that she'd looked him in the eye and told him that she certainly hadn't stolen from this strange woman.

That was all as it should be; he and the other adults of the crew had made a pact when they first took her in that they would try to preserve her innocence, and keep her from as many shady and illegal dealings as possible.

Unless he'd missed something huge, he would trust Ruby's story over Amora's. Which meant that their newcomer was lying.

He leaned forward, meeting Amora's eyes. "Linn tells me that you explained your abrupt arrival on this ship by saying that Ruby had stolen from you, and that you were pursuing her to get back what she took."

"I did tell her that." A moment of hesitation, brief but not brief enough. Amora's eyes skittered away from his. "Because it was the truth."

"Oddly enough, Ruby claims differently." Rodrigo leaned forward, frowning slightly. "In fact, she claims she wasn't doing anything illegal at all, simply returning from an errand she was sent on. Your stories are very nearly opposite, and I think it's only fair to warn you that, of the two of you, I am far more inclined to trust her. So, do you perhaps have any . . . amendments you would like to make to your earlier statements?"

A brief flicker of apprehension crossed Amora's face, but to her credit, she didn't lose her composure. After a long moment of silence, she said slowly, "It's true that I didn't actually see her taking my money. I did see her working her way through the crowd and lifting a few other people's purses, so I thought to check my own. When I discovered it was gone, I naturally assumed it was her work and chased after her. That was pretty much all the coin I had—you can understand my panic."

He could, but he wasn't going to be distracted so easily. "Ruby isn't a thief. I can see how you might *think* she is, given where we are right now, but we've raised her right, even if we're on the wrong side of the law ourselves. She has no reason to go around stealing from anyone—we provide for her just fine and we always have."

"Be that as it may," Amora said evenly, "all I know is what I saw. Perhaps I was mistaken in thinking she'd stolen from me specifically—probably there's some much subtler pickpocket halfway across the city by now who's laughing himself sick at how he got away with my purse. But I saw Ruby, so I chased her and now here I am . . . and while I don't expect that I'm going to get my money back, I would like to go home now, if it's all the same to you."

She was frightened, Rodrigo noticed, frightened and trying to pretend she wasn't. Her poker face was quite good, but he could see the way she'd wrapped her arms around herself, the subtle way she leaned away from him, and the way her eyes darted around the cabin. He had the odd feeling that she wasn't *only* afraid of him and what he might do, but he wasn't sure what else could be scaring her.

"We're not going to kill you," he said at once, reassuringly. "Not unless you try and attack one of us first, which I'm afraid I can't quite see you doing. As for going home . . ." He tried to think through the logistics. "Asad will have taken us high enough by now that we can't just let you down, but we might be able to drop you off in the next day or so. What part of the city are you from?"

Amora's eyes flicked away from him to the scuffed planks of the floor a second time; she was preparing to deflect or lie again. "It doesn't matter," she said. "Wherever you let me down, I should be able to find my way from there."

Rodrigo looked her over, not even trying to be subtle about it. Strange, eye-catching clothes, no shoes (how had she managed to keep up with Ruby, anyway?), hair in a clumsy attempt at a skydweller style, and no money or weapons . . .

He didn't voice the numerous doubts he had about her ability to cross the city on her own, but he knew she got the message anyway.

She glared at him defensively. "What, do you think I have nowhere to go?"

"Do you?"

Amora's defenses held a moment longer before she conceded. "I

. . . technically do," she muttered. "But since someone took most of my money and I'm, um, behind on rent, I might need to . . . find someplace new. And I don't know where that would be, exactly."

The idea that stole upon Rodrigo at that moment was a terrible one. It was something that would likely earn irritated sideways glares from his entire crew for some time, given that Ruby already had reason to dislike Amora, Linn hated when he made decisions without consulting her, Asad always sided with his wife and tended to distrust new people, and Grammy disapproved of most of his olans.

But he couldn't shake the feeling that it was what he ought to do. He could always justify it to Linn as wanting to keep the woman from going to the police. So long as Linn was satisfied, she'd bring the rest of the crew around.

"What is it exactly that you do, Miss Ellis?" he asked casually. Usually this would be something of a rhetorical question, but nothing—from Amora's clothing to her behavior—was giving him the slightest clue.

It took her a second to answer. "I've done a lot of things," she said eventually. "I . . . grew up middle-class, but I've been on my own for some time now. I wouldn't say I'm especially skilled at anything, but I pick things up pretty fast and I get by. I haven't had to take to the sky yet, although I've thought about it a couple of times."

For someone as proud as Amora seemed to be, "getting by" probably translated to what anyone else would call "significant poverty".

Rodrigo had a brief flash of memories of growing up on the street with no one until he met Linn and convinced her to run away from her abusive stepfather. Of the two of them sleeping in doorways and stealing or begging bare necessities until they scraped together enough to get the *Rake* in the air, running on hope and dirt-cheap fuel. Of how they slowly started to make a name for themselves. Of finding Ruby huddled in an alleyway soaking wet, ragged, and bone-thin, and carrying her back to the *Rake* wrapped in his coat. Of the following months they spent convincing her that she really was going to be cared for from now on.

He had a bad habit of taking in strays and lost causes, for no other reason than that they needed it. If he did so now, it would definitely get him in trouble—they had more than enough crew already, they couldn't afford another mouth to feed, and they knew very little about this woman, meaning she could turn into a significant liability.

But Amora was alone and frightened, and more than that, she had a well of stubbornness in her that he couldn't help but admire. And she'd didn't seem to view criminal work as something unthinkable, which was promising.

He found himself saying, "Given that you seem to need a place to go and it'd be more trouble to get you off the ship than to keep you—" A lie, but who needed to know that? "—I was thinking of offering you a job. Have you ever worked in a galley? Grammy's technically got it covered, but she's not as young as she once was, and she could probably use the assistance."

Amora hesitated for a moment, but after a silent struggle she finally said, "I haven't cooked for anyone but myself before, but that doesn't mean I can't learn. It's not as though I have any better choices, and I've definitely done worse work."

"Good. If you know the basics, you should do fine. I'll talk to her about it and see what arrangements can be made." He stood and reached out to shake her hand. "Welcome aboard, Miss Amora."

She shook the hand he extended but grimaced slightly. "I, um, prefer Ellis, actually."

"Ellis it is, then." Rodrigo moved towards the door, gesturing for her to follow. "Come on. We'd best stick together for explaining to Grammy that I've saddled her with an assistant."

With Ellis more properly introduced to Grammy—something which happened much more smoothly than he was expecting—Rodrigo found himself wandering the ship aimlessly. Well, not technically aimlessly—he knew what he needed to do, but he didn't want to do it. As the afternoon wore on to the dinner hour, though, he forced himself to snap out of it. This needed to be cleared up now, before it came to a head in front of the whole crew.

When he finally sought her out, Ruby was assiduously and all-too-innocently scrubbing laundry out on the deck. Rodrigo took a seat on a nearby coil of rope and waited for her to acknowledge his presence.

Finally, she looked up and asked, "Is something wrong?"

"I confess I'm not sure," Rodrigo said slowly. "I've spoken with Miss Ellis, and while she admits that she may have been mistaken about you being the one to lift her purse, she swears that she saw you pickpocketing several other people down below."

"She can't prove anything," Ruby said, but she wasn't meeting his eyes.

An obvious tell, and one that made his heart sink. Rodrigo sighed. "I know she can't prove anything, and it is essentially her word against yours. But I don't think she was lying." He shifted forward and lowered his voice. "You're not in trouble, Ruby. I just want to know why you did it."

"No reason." But she was still not looking him in the eye.

"That's not going to work, because I know there was a reason. You're not someone who just steals for your own amusement."

"You say that like that's not what you do all the time."

"What?" Rodrigo shook his head, confused. "No, I don't. I steal because that's the best way I know to keep the *Rake* flying and to keep us all fed and supplied. And with the way I do it, the only people who lose anything are those who have enough to lose. Not people like Ellis who have to keep everything they have on them, and are left with no options if someone takes that."

"I said I didn't steal from her. I'd have remembered—she was dressed strangely enough."

"I believe that much. I'm saying that the ones you did steal from could have been just like her." Ruby didn't bother denying the assertion this time.

Rodrigo ran a hand through his tied-back hair in frustration. "But even more than that, I'm trying to tell you that that isn't safe. When Linn and I go on a heist, we know what we're doing and we have backup plans and escape routes in case something goes wrong. If you're down there by yourself with nobody knowing what you're up to, something terrible could happen to you and we wouldn't be able to help. It might seem like some glamorous adventure —"

"I'm not a child," Ruby interrupted. "I know it's dangerous. But I want to help. I'm fifteen—I'm old enough to bring in some money for the crew and to contribute. Linn says she was younger than I am now when she ran away with you."

So, he might need to talk to Linn about this, too. He assumed she didn't actually know about these escapades—considering she'd agreed with him when they took Ruby in that they were going to try and raise her as respectably as possible under the circumstances—but if she had known, and had even encouraged Ruby, then there was clearly something amiss.

He stood and rested a hand on Ruby's shoulder. "You might think you're grown up, but it's my job to make sure we're provided for—that's why I'm the captain. So, you don't need to go out pickpocketing again."

"Yessir."

"Promise you won't go looking for trouble like that again?"

There was a long moment of silence before Ruby finally said, "I promise."

There was something about the way she said it that seemed off, but he shook the feeling away. She had promised after all, and if he couldn't trust his crew, who could he trust?

That, and he had plenty of other things to worry about with the newest addition to their crew.

Chapter 5

Latisha supposed she should be panicking.

She was inexplicably in a world that, somehow, was based on her novels, and when she'd been offered a job that would keep her in close proximity to Rodrigo—someone she'd told herself she needed to stay away from—she'd accepted it instead of running for the hills.

Not to mention that she was by now very sure that none of this was a dream or some kind of coma-induced hallucination. By all accounts, it was definitely time to panic.

She would have, too, except that she was sure that there had to be some way out of this. She'd read enough books growing up about kids getting pulled into fantasy worlds and having adventures, and they always went home at the end. It was even part of that hero's journey thing everyone had made countless graphs of.

Eventually, whatever had happened to make her end up here would reverse itself, and working on the *Rake* was just the easiest way to survive until then.

Grammy, who had accepted her as an assistant far more quickly than Latisha would have expected, was showing her around the galley. It was a square, slightly cramped room adjacent to the mess, with cupboards and kitchen equipment lining all four walls and a distinct smell of old meals that the tiny open window did nothing to mitigate.

"The stove needs a couple of good whacks just here," Grammy instructed, tapping a spot on the right side of the slightly askew, smoking black box, "before it'll do anything useful. Don't worry about the icebox clattering; it just does that sometimes. The sink drain clogs every now and again, but you needn't worry about running the water too much, 'cause Asad finally got a distillery running, and we pull what we need out of the air now. The bread machine —" She gestured at a slightly dented brass appliance with several jointed arms sticking out of its shell. "— is by no means to be left unsupervised while it's working. There's a box of recipe cards on that counter and a rationing chart tacked on that cupboard—I'll help you along until you figure them out. The one straightforward thing is coffee." Grammy tapped a gleaming golden contraption that looked like a cross between a samovar and a very early prototype of an espresso machine. "This hasn't ever broken down, not for lack of some people's trying, and coffee's the one thing Linn won't grumble about us taking extra of."

As much of a relief as that was, Latisha's attention had snagged on something else. "I thought Rodrigo was in charge. Is Linn the . . . co-captain, or something?"

"Nah, she's first mate. Still his better half in a lot of ways, and of the two of them, she's the one we can rely on to be practical when he's gone fopping off again."

Latisha did her best to feign confusion—after all, there was a chance she might be wrong. "Are they married? I thought —"

Grammy snorted with laughter. "She's married to Asad. The engineer-navigator, you'd have seen him earlier. Doesn't stop her from holding onto the captain's brain for him when he leaves it behind."

She turned away, and Latisha seized the opportunity to try and trip over nothing at all. A fall had gotten her here, so perhaps a fall would get her out. Unfortunately, all that happened was that she ended up sprawled on her hands and knees on the scrubbed-smooth floor.

"That won't do you any good," Grammy commented, looking down at her, but before Latisha could even fully startle, the older woman's expression seemed to twitch, and she continued, "Come on, up you get. The busier you keep, the quicker the others'll stop thinking of you as captain's new stray and take to you."

Latisha gripped Grammy's gnarled hand to pull herself up. She would just ignore the odd moment, and insist to herself that nothing unusual had been said.

Over the following couple of hours, Latisha did what she could to assist with the overly-complicated task that was dinner—how was it so difficult to throw together a shepherd's pie ?

Luckily, under Grammy's terse supervision, nothing caught fire and it looked like the meal would be edible.

Of course, that was when Latisha realized she would have to be in the same room as Rodrigo again. She almost considered begging off and trying to go to bed (somewhere) early, but in the end, hunger won out over the desire to hide.

As they all gathered around the table, she noted she needn't have worried. Rodrigo seemed to be carefully not paying attention to her, in much the same way that he and Linn were being carefully polite to each other—as she'd once written they did after they'd just had an argument.

Ruby and Asad kept watching her sideways like they expected her to morph into some deranged saboteur at any moment. Latisha might have been bothered by that, if she hadn't been preoccupied with surprise that Asad actually ate food. She supposed she'd mentioned him being present at meals before, despite being an automaton, and she'd never come out and said just what he used for fuel (although, if memory served, her old notes specified "just about anything combustible").

She was startled out of her thoughts by Linn saying abruptly, "Grammy, will you need Ellis for cleanup tonight, or do you mind if I borrow her to get her situated?"

31

Judging by the subtle but immediate relaxation in Rodrigo's posture, this signaled some kind of truce. "Go right ahead," Grammy responded. "Is she sharing with me and Ruby?"

"We cleared out the storage room," Asad spoke up. "There wasn't much in there to begin with. It doesn't have a window, but you'll be the only one besides Rodrigo without a cabin mate."

"I can always share with her if you want your own space again," Linn commented, one eyebrow lifted in a clear tease.

"She should be so lucky."

"The storage room should be fine," Latisha jumped in. "Thank you." As she spoke, Asad seemed to draw back into himself slightly, the sparks raised by the banter quickly dying out.

Dinner finished shortly afterward, and she was quick to follow Linn from the galley. They made their way down the corridor and eventually right to where Latisha expected — a small room near the stern.

It was smaller than the galley — just over half the size — but there was also a lot less in it, containing only a cot, a dimly burning oil lamp, and a small open trunk at the foot of the cot that appeared to have folded clothes in it.

Somehow, the clothes implied just a little too much permanence, and Latisha found herself saying, "I won't need the trunk. I can just wear what I have on."

Linn gave her a look. "You must not have gone high before, or you'd know — if you try to walk around dressed like that, on a skyship, in February, you will regret it. You might've stayed warm in the galley so far, but you can't always be in there."

Ah, right. It tends to get a lot colder at these altitudes, she abruptly remembered. *Permanence or not, I'd rather avoid freezing to death.*

"See if you can find anything that fits," Linn continued. "If something doesn't, let me know tomorrow and I might be able to help you alter it."

Then she left, just as Latisha was working out that the clothes had likely belonged to Linn. She should have thanked her . . . or

32

something.

Now that she was finally alone, she could feel the adrenaline draining out of her, and it was all she could do to pull the door the rest of the way closed and flop down onto the cot.

"There's no place like home," she mumbled, tapping her still-bare heels together three times. Nothing happened, not that she was expecting it to.

Still, she kept on trying out every variation of, "I wish I were back home," that she could think of until she fell asleep.

It turned out that sleeping and waking up wasn't the magic solution either.

Latisha groaned as she woke up stiff and sore from sleeping in her jeans, face pressed into a pillowcase that smelled of lye soap and a hint of smoke. Everything on the *Rake*—\or maybe in the whole world—seemed to smell a little bit like smoke.

It was, now that she was paying attention, noticeably cold, so she gave in and rummaged in the trunk for something she could stand to wear. There were a few combination undergarments, three pairs of thick stockings, two blouses (one cream-colored, one ecru), two skirts in different shades of brown, and three heavy corsets that Latisha was . . . mostly sure were supposed to go over the blouses, rather than under—the blouses were too form-fitting to work any other way. There was also an assortment of random belts at the bottom of the trunk, a pair of high-heeled black leather boots under the cot, and a packet of hairpins tangled up in one of the skirts.

It was quite clear, on investigation, why Linn had donated these —she tended to favor a more practical dress style that featured pants and high-collared blouses, plus her ever-present coat. None of these garments fit very well with that style; they were much more similar to something a truly headache-inducing fan would wear while proclaiming her undying love for Rodrigo at a book signing.

Still, it could have been worse, Latisha decided, taking it all in. She could have fallen in with higher-class characters somewhere, who cared a lot more about getting the details of dress etiquette exactly right. Skydwellers, from what she remembered, were rather more creative about such things, so probably no one would bat an eye if she got something hilariously wrong.

She still cursed repeatedly as she tried to work out the buckles and laces and buttons of the assorted garments and wished heartily that she'd invented a sci-fi world instead. Perhaps she would have been able to write the stories she wanted to write, then, instead of having to turn it into a setting for cheap romances. And even if she hadn't, the characters would have all been in jumpsuits, or maybe even t-shirts and pants.

An impromptu visit to that kind of world would have been a lot less frustrating.

In the end, she managed to put something together involving the white blouse (ruffled and with far too low a V-neckline for comfort), a dark brown corset over that, a skirt made partially out of the same material and partially out of some flowing ecru stuff and lace, and a belt. The boots turned out to be easier to walk in than she'd expected, meaning that she didn't trip and fall within the first two minutes, but she was still scratching her head as to the practicality of them. How did anyone run around a ship and heist and fence and so on in these things?

By the end of the day, though, Latisha realized that she'd almost forgotten she wasn't in her usual clothes. Her new outfit was, somehow, insidiously comfortable.

She decided that she resented this ridiculous state of affairs and repeated her routine of wishing fervently into her pillow when she fell into bed that night.

It still didn't have any effect, and it kept on not having any effect night after night. None of the cupboard or cabin doors she opened ever led anywhere except where they were supposed to, and pinching herself only gave her a bruise that Grammy frowned questioningly at.

One evening, she even stole a stub pencil and a recipe card for black pudding that Grammy never touched and scribbled on the back of it: *The next morning, Latisha Robbins, aka Amora Ellis, woke up at home.* That didn't work either, but then nothing she tried writing down came true, whether it was, *There was pie for dinner the next day,* or *Rodrigo has pink hair now.*

The only other thing Latisha could think to try was retracing her steps to where she'd first arrived in the world, but she had no idea where that spot had been or how to get back to it. She might have invented the city, but her mental map of it was nowhere near that good.

Several nights later, when she finally arrived at the realization that she was well and truly stuck, panic finally set in. She was trapped here, surrounded by everything she hated. She was going to have to spend the rest of her life in corsets, skirts, and heels, on Rodrigo's stupid flying ship, living off the windfalls from his stupid, stupid seduction heists.

Who even knew how long she would live, with all the smoke in the air here? It was a wonder she hadn't been coughing up her lungs. Not to mention that there was a non-zero chance of them all being apprehended and thrown in some prison to rot.

Instead of wishing, Latisha cried in frustration into her pillow until she fell asleep.

When morning came, irritation was already simmering under Latisha's skin.

Encountering a sizable knot as she tried to put her hair up for the day seemed like the final straw. There hadn't been much she could do in the way of upkeep in the past couple of weeks, besides finger-combing and washing it with the same soap that was available to wash the rest of her. That hadn't done anything to combat how dry and brittle her curls were becoming at this higher altitude, and tangles had been getting harder and harder to fight.

Ordinarily, something like this wouldn't have fazed her. Now, though, she was trapped in a world that was all of her greatest mistakes, regrets, and irritations brought to life, and she couldn't even make something as normal as doing her hair go right.

Someone was knocking at her door—probably Grammy wanting to know what was keeping her. Latisha crossed the tiny room in three strides and yanked the door open, fully prepared with a snappish retort—

It wasn't Grammy, though. Ruby was standing there, looking nervous but determined, and holding a glass jar half-full of an off-white substance.

"What?" Latisha demanded. Curiosity was replacing her earlier annoyance, however. Ruby had barely tolerated her company so far, and certainly had never sought her out.

"I'm right next door, and the walls are pretty thin. I heard you muttering," Ruby explained.

Right. Latisha had been doing some of that towards the end, and a little swearing.

"It's a detangling problem, right?" Ruby went on. She tapped the jar. "This stuff helps. I can share, if you want."

Perhaps Latisha should have thought of such a solution before, since Ruby's short cloud of hair never seemed to give her grief. Still, she found herself saying, "I didn't know you had something like that—" *In this world,* she almost finished, but caught herself in time. "—on this ship. Grammy mentioned that the budget was a little tight."

Ruby shrugged. "When I first started living here, we didn't. Everybody kept taking turns trying to do my hair, but they mostly just made things worse. Grammy finally came up with something that didn't cost much to make, and that did the trick."

Latisha thought about asking how on earth Grammy had known how to make hair product, but decided that that wasn't the real question at hand. "Why are you helping me?" she asked instead. "Last time I checked, you didn't like me too much."

"I don't trust you, at least not yet," Ruby clarified. "But you haven't done anything bad so far, and it looks like you're going to stick around, so we should probably get used to each other. There's not enough space on the *Rake* to avoid each other all the time."

She gestured at the doorway. "Can I come in?"

Latisha stepped aside to let her pass. After a little negotiation, they ended up both sitting on the cot, Latisha in front and Ruby working the stuff from the jar into her wet hair. Refreshingly, it smelled sweet and clean, like apple blossoms.

It had been some time since anyone else had played with Latisha's hair, and the feeling relaxed her enough to try and make conversation. "So, what was the book on your bunk about? I saw something there, but I didn't get a good look."

Ruby hummed. "Nothing. An adventure story I, um, found."

"I would've thought you were living in one of those already," Latisha commented.

"This is just getting by," Ruby said dismissively. "Lots of people live like this. A real adventure would be . . . climbing a mountain that's never been explored, or flying around the world, or going to the moon."

Latisha was torn between amusement at the teenager's casual attitude towards living on a flying ship, and amazement that Ruby seemed to be opening up a little. "I suppose you have a point." A pause. "Which would you pick, if you had to pick one?"

"The moon," was the immediate response. "Nobody's ever done it, and everyone has a different idea of what's up there. In *Lunar Holiday*, there's bat people who live in caves, but in *Stars and Stockings*, there are these cities made of crystal . . ."

By the time Latisha's hair was tangle-free and put into a plait that twisted neatly into a bun, Ruby had considerably warmed up to her. She departed, profusely thanked, with the promise to share her own supply of conditioner until Latisha could get her own.

As she made her way to the galley, Latisha's mind was on

something besides hair and dime novels. If she were going to be stuck here indefinitely, she was only going to make things worse for herself if she kept avoiding everyone but Grammy. Something needed to change, and as Ruby had just demonstrated, connecting with the rest of the crew wasn't impossible.

She was nearly late to help serve breakfast, although Grammy didn't question where she'd been. After the meal, there was a full slate of chores waiting, but for once, Latisha didn't mind.

That would just give her time to plan.

Chapter 6

Rodrigo had known that there would be a certain adjustment period during Ellis' first few days on the *Rake*.

There always was with someone new. Linn hadn't counted — she'd been there since before the ship was anything more than a street kid's dream of jam tomorrow — but everyone else who'd come after had changed the dynamic subtly and irrevocably.

Asad had been the first, and he'd been the third wheel to Rodrigo and Linn's well-oiled partnership right up until he wasn't, and Rodrigo turned around to find himself the third wheel to something else entirely. He'd also shifted things in that now they had someone on board who weren't just in danger from the law, but also from fellow skydwellers who thought that a lack of blood made him less of a person.

Ruby had changed *everything*, because she was the first one who was there primarily to live, rather than to work — the first one whom they actively tried to keep out of their illegal dealings. And Grammy . . . she was just strange. She'd marched up to them at the docks one day, right past the hired toughs that scared off police and most everyone else, and announced she was going to run galley for them and that was that. They'd been uneasy around her for months, sure this was part of a scheme by someone they'd ticked off in the past. But nothing had happened, and none of them had wanted to go back to the days when no one on board could produce palatable food, so eventually, she'd become one of them.

Rodrigo kept watching and waiting for the same thing to happen with Ellis, but for the first fortnight, it was clear that she was still somehow separate. It wasn't just down to the crew not accepting her—they were still a little wary, but Ellis seemed to be at least as wary of them. She held herself apart, and even though they were all living in fairly tight quarters, it felt like she was barely there.

He tried to not make it obvious that he was paying attention; after he'd gone over everyone else's heads to hire her, he didn't need to make it look like he was playing favorites. But he did keep an eye on her, because if this didn't work out, Linn was going to take great delight in proclaiming that she'd told him so, and that was never enjoyable.

And then one day, it was like someone had thrown a switch, and everything changed.

He noticed it first with Ruby.

The cabin girl tended to spend her free time tucked into some odd corner with one of her paperbacks—not that she had *much* free time, since she'd never quite shaken the habit of working as much as possible from when she was new and thought she had to earn her place.

But now, for no reason that Rodrigo could discern, it was becoming more common to see her chatting with Ellis on occasion. Their new addition apparently had a fondness for books to match Ruby's, and from what he could gather, this seemed to be how they were winning each other over. Supposedly, Ruby hadn't actually lent Ellis one of her precious novels, but the possibility existed, which was as much as could be said for anyone on the crew.

It made sense, he concluded. Grammy and Ruby were traditionally the ones who were shipbound the most, and it looked like Ellis would be the same. Unless they were planning to destroy the ship with their mutual discomfort, some kind of accord would have to be reached.

Rodrigo was kept busy, venturing around the city to collect information on Lady Jennifer, to establish his flimsy false identity, and to win her favor enough to secure a ball invitation sometime soon.

But when he was on the *Rake*, he caught little moments: Ruby going to mop the deck, and Ellis approaching and offering to help, not seeming to mind when she was rebuffed. Ruby taking less food than she should, again, and getting into an argument with Linn about it, while Ellis used the distraction to make up the difference from her own plate. Ellis' cabin door being open when he got up early one morning, and her and Ruby's voices coming from inside, talking about . . . hair, it sounded like.

The next time he caught Ruby alone, he mentioned, "You seem to have forgiven Ellis for revealing your escapade earlier."

Ruby tilted her head thoughtfully. "I didn't mind that. She was doing what she figured she needed to do. I just thought she might be here to make trouble, but she hasn't tried anything yet. I think . . . she might have been as nervous about us as we were about her."

Asad was the next, which made perfect sense and was surprising at the same time.

It was surprising because most people didn't like automata, claiming different reasons that all really boiled down to "they're not human". Verne models such as Asad had it better than most. Because they were made for engineering and navigation, their sentience was more obvious, meaning that they were more likely to be treated as coworkers instead of objects by the humans their manufacturer contracted them out to. They could choose surnames and refuse some jobs and marry humans, which wasn't true for all models.

Even so, Asad was slow to warm up to people outside the crew until they'd earned it. Unfortunately, not many people did.

And yet, it still made sense for Ellis to approach him next. At

41

face value, after Grammy and Ruby, Asad was the least threatening person on the crew. It wasn't that he wasn't capable— even dangerous—when the situation called for it. It was just that under normal circumstances, he was about as far from menacing as it was possible for a professional criminal to get.

When Linn, fed up with the *Rake* constantly breaking down, had spent their remaining savings on a Verne contract, Rodrigo had had his doubts. There was no way someone like that, human or automaton, who had never even bent the law or been in a fight before, could be useful to them. The only reason Asad had stayed was because he'd explained his only other option was to contract with a freighter captain notorious for returning automata with "accidental" damage. Rodrigo' soft spot for desperate causes had made itself known, and he'd given into the inevitable and hired him.

Several months later, he was fleeing from a mark's home, her five-generations-old diamond tiara clutched in one hand and the rope ladder in the other, only to find that his expected cover fire wasn't coming. Turned out that Linn had gotten cut by the broken window on her dominant arm and couldn't fire back at the mark's fiancé—who, of course, was an officer—and his army friends. Asad, however, had appeared over the railing and covered them with a rifle they hadn't even known was on the ship until they could clamber aboard. The rifle, it turned out, was of Asad's own design—his previous contract had been with a custom firearms maker.

Rodrigo had had to confess himself impressed, even if it took him a while to work around to saying it after Linn hauled Asad in for a drawn-out kiss right then and there.

Ellis wasn't to know about that, though, and she didn't seem to mind that he was an automaton. She kept on trying to draw him into conversation about the engine mechanics or some detail of life on the *Rake*, but her overtures only caused him to spend less and less time in the mess or other places she might be.

Today, though, he caught up to Rodrigo after dinner and caught his elbow. "Captain," he said quietly and evenly. "There's something we need to discuss."

Rodrigo blinked. "Something, as in . . ."

"Ellis has been hanging around in the engine room," Asad elaborated. "Not a lot, just when she has free time from the galley, but she keeps asking how things work."

"Have you tried asking her why?" Rodrigo ventured. "Perhaps she's just interested in machinery."

"She says she's 'curious'," Asad said skeptically, as if no one could ever be trusted to simply be curious about something. "She hasn't tried to fiddle with anything yet, but she keeps on looking at me like she wants to apologize for something. Like she wants me to trust her." He hesitated. "Shouldn't we be concerned that she might try to sabotage the ship?"

That didn't seem remotely in line with what, admittedly little, Rodrigo had picked up about her. "Why would she do that?"

Asad shrugged. "Why else would she keep coming to talk to me?"

Which, as little as Rodrigo liked to admit it, was a fair enough question with the world and Asad being what they were.

He promised to look into it, and the next time he caught Ellis on her own, he pulled her aside and asked as unthreateningly as possible, "Any particular reason you keep visiting the engine room?"

She looked a little surprised, but rallied, pulling away from him just a tiny bit. "I think it's interesting. I never had the chance to find out how skyships work before, and now I can. Is that a problem?"

Her answer was guileless enough that Rodrigo didn't think it would be a problem, but for his navigator's sake, he answered, "Asad was just a bit . . . wary, is all."

"He's nice. I wish he didn't feel like he needed to hide from me."

Then she was gone, continuing on her way.

Rodrigo wasn't sure exactly what happened after that, but perhaps the conversation inspired Ellis to say something to Asad, or perhaps he decided to get used to her. All he knew was that, at dinner the next day, Ellis started talking with Asad about a fault that the bread machine had developed, and in another minute he was talking with her about repairs, carrying on a conversation beyond the one- or two-word responses that were all he'd spoken to her at meals since she arrived.

Asking how it had happened would probably do more harm than good, so he kept his mouth shut and pretended he hadn't noticed anything at all.

He also ignored that the others were all exchanging sharp, surprised looks.

After Asad came Linn. She had forgiven Rodrigo for hiring yet another crew member without telling her—even though there had been some shouting along the way, they couldn't manage to stay angry at each other for long. The setting up of Ellis' makeshift cabin had been something of a peace offering, but Linn's olive branch was still a good distance from her actually liking someone.

Once it became clear that Ellis was going to get along with and look out for Ruby, that was one significant step, and her slowly earning Asad's trust was another. Linn would never fully warm up to anyone who feared or disrespected her husband, and the two of them had never been subtle in their parental attitudes towards Ruby.

Once that had been achieved, Rodrigo knew to watch for small, subtle signs: Grammy mentioning that Ellis had made the evening's hot pot on her own and Linn saying, "It's good," offhandedly when she usually wouldn't say anything, Ellis wondering aloud if there was a way to install a lock for her door and Linn offering to help her since Asad was wrapped up in a project, and—most importantly—Linn telling him in passing one

44

evening that they should probably make sure Ellis had a knife to carry with her in case she needed to run an errand on the ground sometime.

"I take it you're all right with her staying around, then," he said in response, too pleased to even really feel the need for an "I told you so".

Linn just gave a small smile. "I know what your bad decisions tend to look like, and she isn't one of them."

Maybe it was because of that assessment that Rodrigo wasn't too concerned about Ellis reading his whole crew so well that she could figure out just how to best befriend them all. He probably should have put a little more thought into how it was almost like she knew them all, but he couldn't focus on that, being occupied with something else entirely.

Ellis had sought out every other denizen of the *Rake*, except for him.

It wasn't as though he were somehow hurt by it—that would be ridiculous. It was just rather strange, and no matter how he tried, he couldn't come up with an explanation for it. He couldn't think of anything he might have done to frighten or offend her. It couldn't be that she was generally wary of men considering she got along with Asad splendidly. It couldn't be what he did for a living, or she wouldn't have stayed this long, let alone taken to the others as much as she had.

Rodrigo was aware, of course, that Ellis didn't need a reason to not want to be around him, but in his experience, people had reasons for the things they did. He wanted to know what Ellis' was for avoiding him, and why she was so trepidatious when they did cross paths. If nothing else, for professional reasons, so that he could avoid the same thing happening with a mark someday.

He pondered it perhaps rather more than he should have, very nearly losing his focus when he should have had his full attention on Lady Jennifer's invitation to a ball at her townhome.

Of course, then a much more significant problem entered the picture.

Chapter 7

The morning that disaster struck started out not all that differently from any other morning since Latisha had arrived on the *Rake*.

She woke sometime around dawn, suppressed a yelp of horror as she remembered where she was—although lately it had been more of a resigned sigh—fumbled her way through the hooks and buttons and laces of her clothes for the day, and shuffled to the galley for some of Grammy's strong black coffee.

"Mm," she muttered into a steaming mug of the stuff, blinking to keep her eyelids from sticking back together. "The presence of caffeine is the one thing I got right about this stupid world."

Grammy, a few feet away, gave her a long look that Latisha's foggy mind couldn't interpret, but didn't say anything.

Once she was more alert and in the midst of making breakfast, however, it occurred to her that the *Rake* was far too quiet even for this hour of the morning. There were faint sounds of the engines running down below, of Ruby doing her morning chores, and nothing from Rodrigo, who always slept in later than anyone, the lout, but . . .

"Where have Linn and Asad gotten to?" she asked Grammy, looking up from the porridge she was stirring. "Usually, I can hear them up and about by now."

"They went out on an errand sometime before dawn," Grammy said briefly. "They'll be back in a bit."

Latisha wanted to ask what kind of errand, and why they would need to leave before dawn, but something in Grammy's tone made her decide against it. She'd find out when they got back, after all.

In this moment, she needed to focus on not letting the porridge turn into glop.

Asad and Linn came back just as breakfast was being dished out. Asad looked tired and like he was recovering from being severely frightened, and Linn was carrying a messenger bag and walking with a limp.

"I twisted my ankle getting off that roof," she snapped when Ruby started to ask her about it. "Go get Grammy and tell her to get the medical supplies and meet me in my cabin. Is Rodrigo up yet?"

"No. He's probably still dead to the world at this hour," Latisha contributed.

Linn huffed. "Well, that's something, at least. Hopefully we can get this taken care of quickly so he doesn't notice."

"You've sprained your ankle. You'll need to take it easy for a week at least," Asad pointed out. "Just tell him you tripped going down one of the ship's ladders, or something."

"I don't *trip* on ladders."

"Yes, well, Rodrigo's fairly gullible. He won't question it."

To get Linn below decks, somebody had to take the bulky messenger bag while somebody else helped the injured woman. Ruby ended up with the former job, which left Latisha with the job of navigating Linn's descent down the ladder. Linn wasn't the sort to accept much help, and she ended up doing most of it under her own power, which was good in some ways—if Latisha had had to support her weight they probably would have both fallen over— but bad in that Linn kept hissing with pain every time she put weight on her right foot.

Grammy clucked and frowned when she saw the injury, "You're going to have to tell the captain something, that's for sure," she said firmly. "You're supposed to go with him to Lady Jennifer's ball in a few days, but you're not going to be able to dance on that, not unless you want to injure it worse."

"I'll deal with it," Linn said shortly. "Lady Jennifer's not like his usual twits. She's actually got a brain. I'm not letting him walk in there alone, he'd be bound to do something stupid and reckless. Or don't you remember the Erdensohn job?"

Latisha did. The novel in question, *Moonstone Fair*, had ended with the revelation that the mark, Brigitte Erdensohn, was so deeply superstitious about the healing properties of the moonstone Rodrigo was trying to steal that if it were lost, she would have an attack of hypochondria and panic herself to death. Latisha had planned for him to take the pendant anyway and give up his life of crime due to crippling guilt, but her editor Evie had made her end it with him not completing the heist, meaning that the crew had to organize another job quickly to pay off the debts that the moonstone was supposed to cover.

It had been the exact opposite of what Latisha had been trying to achieve, and she had, in fact, needed to write Linn out of that whole sequence: the more practical first mate would never have let him get away with such a rash move.

Since she wasn't supposed to know about any of that, however, she kept her mouth shut.

Grammy, for some reason, glanced over at her anyway, before turning back to Linn. "Let me talk to the captain about it," she said. "You can't lie to him outright to save your life. Goodness knows how you've kept secrets from him so long. And you," she said, turning to Asad, "had better go out and get me more horse chestnut as soon as you can, because we were running low before and we'll be out within the day now. Fence whatever's in that bag that I don't want to know about, if you need to."

Asad nodded, and Grammy added, almost as an afterthought, "Might as well take Ellis with you. It's about time she knows what goes on around here, and some things it's easier to show than tell."

The part of the city where they were let down was a little less upscale than the area where Latisha had first emerged. The streets were narrower, and the buildings were smaller, more packed together, and much less ornamented. Almost all of them had cheap eateries or dingy shops on the ground floors, with apartments situated above.

To her credit, Latisha refrained from exploding with questions until she and Asad were on their way down the street, and even then she kept her voice in an undertone. "All right, what's going on? Where did you and Linn go? Why did it have to be so early? How did she get hurt? And why was Grammy talking about a fence?"

Asad let out a long breath, looking this way and that as they walked. "So, you know that Rodrigo heists jewelry and such from those young women he's always after, right? And you know about Ruby's pickpocketing."

"Yes."

"Rodrigo doesn't know about the pickpocketing," Asad said bluntly. "Or rather, he didn't until he found out from you, but he still doesn't know the real reason for it. He tried to make her promise she would stop, although I'm pretty sure she managed a loophole. He has some noble idea that he can keep her all youthful and innocent, even though she's living on a boat full of thieves. Which would be nice, but unfortunately, it just isn't practical."

"But . . ." Latisha tried to process. "I thought what Rodrigo does —the heists—aren't those how you make money?"

Asad laughed, but not in a happy way. "*He* thinks so. If it was just him and Linn—and maybe Ruby—it might even work. But those shiny little trinkets aren't actually worth as much as he thinks, especially the really distinctive ones that everybody knows are stolen. Those one-of-a-kind ones are, unfortunately, the ones he has a weakness for, too."

Latisha shifted uncomfortably. Technically, *she'd* been responsible for having the crew steal such fabulous and recognizable bits of jewelry over the years—it sounded better in print to say you were heisting a centuries-old heirloom called the "Gloaming Pendant" than to say you'd nicked someone's ordinary sapphire necklace.

It wasn't very realistic, but that had never bothered her or anyone else.

Before Asad could continue, they arrived at a small and dingy shop that looked like exactly what it was—a sketchy pawnbroker's. The sign over the shop read MONACHUS in peeling painted letters. Everything inside was covered in a fine layer of dust.

A bell dinged as the door swung shut behind them, and a scrawny, hunched bald man in an outsized, grimy black coat appeared behind the counter. "Mr. Hafidi," he uttered in oily tones. "And a different companion today, I see. Did your . . . wife finally sell your contract? Or is this a temporary arrangement, one that is more covert, perhaps?"

Latisha wanted to splutter and snap at the man, first for suggesting that either Linn or Asad would betray the other like that, and then for implying that she would be in a relationship with someone she'd invented. There had to be something wrong with anyone as narcissistic as that, right?

Asad, however, reacted calmly. "Linn has other business today, Monachus. Business that is none of yours." He opened the messenger bag and began taking things out, arranging them on the counter. "And if you want what I'm selling, you'll keep a civil tongue when it comes to my marriage."

Latisha couldn't help staring at the things he was casually laying out on the dirty wooden counter. Necklaces, earrings, bracelets, and rings that glittered in the dim light—nothing with a family crest or any other identifying marks, nothing too expensive, but all of it clearly valuable. Judging by the poorly concealed glint in his eyes, Monachus' attention had been caught as well.

"Quite the haul," he observed, picking up one of the bracelets and playing with it. "And one or two that are even rather old,

51

although the workmanship is shoddy on a few. I'll give you three hundred in gold for the lot."

Asad actually snorted. "You've been dealing with me for this long and you still think you can put one over on me? Seven hundred."

They carried on bargaining and bickering for a few minutes more, with Monachus eventually conceding to paying five hundred when Asad seemed close to losing his temper. The pawnbroker swept the treasure into a box that was promptly squirreled away. He then counted out the money into a pouch that Asad took with uncharacteristic grimness.

Once they were safely away, Asad let out a long, shuddering breath and leaned against a nearby wall.

Latisha hovered, uncertain of what to do.

"Are you . . . is everything all right?" she finally asked.

Asad kept breathing raggedly in and out, one hand fidgeting with the interlocked rings he wore on a cord around his neck—the wedding rings that matched Linn's. "Yes. Sorry. It usually goes better than that—I could've gotten another fifty out of him if I'd held it together. I just—Linn said she got injured coming off a rooftop, but she underplayed it. She always does. She *fell.*"

Latisha swallowed hard at the sheer pain in his voice.

"She was hanging onto the edge of the roof and I had to pull her back without falling myself," Asad continued, "and at the time I couldn't really panic about it. But she could have died. Stupidly, for no reason. And I—don't know what I would've done."

Latisha didn't know what to say. She tried putting a comforting hand on the man's shoulder, but it didn't seem to make a difference.

"Meeting her on the *Rake* changed my life," he went on, "She really is the best thing to ever happen to me and I don't know what I would do without her. And she almost died for that haul and Monachus was acting like it was nothing . . . which he always does, and he wasn't to know, but . . ." Asad scrubbed a hand

52

through his hair, clearly frustrated. " And Rodrigo, he's a good man, and the best boss I've had . . ."

"But it bothers you when Linn's first concern after getting hurt is how it'll affect *him*, rather than being worried about her own well-being," Latisha finished.

"Yes." Asad looked at her curiously. "Yes, that's it. I hadn't thought about it that way, but you're right."

He took a deep breath, and turned to continue down the street, Latisha following. There wasn't much else she could do but continue on after him, what with everything he'd just unloaded on her. She hadn't bothered to consider the smaller details of the *Rake* crew, but now that she was seeing their struggles firsthand, something painful and tight was beginning to twist in her chest.

Unaware of her thoughts, Asad started speaking over his shoulder. "So anyway, now you know what really keeps us in the air," he said conversationally, as if he hadn't come close to breaking down a moment ago. "Linn and I slip away when we can —when Rodrigo won't find out—and we steal things that'll actually bring in some money. Wealthy older women are the best. They've accumulated more jewels than they know what to do with, and they usually won't miss the amount that we take. Between that and Ruby's pickpocketing, we get by, but it can get tight sometimes. Rodrigo's heists help, but they also put us all at risk even more."

"And then I show up," Latisha guessed, "and Rodrigo insists on keeping me around even though I'm an extra mouth to feed and I can't really contribute, and I'm also one more person you have to keep secrets from."

"Well, there shouldn't be any more secrets left after this," Asad pointed out, "and I'm sure you'll find some way to help balance things out. Give it time. You haven't even been around for a month yet."

With that, he led her into an apothecary's in search of horse chestnut, but Latisha's mind was spinning. This trip had given her a lot of answers, but some of them weren't answers she was sure she wanted. The more time she spent in this world, the more cracks she discovered in what she'd thought to be a fairly ideal arrangement. And those cracks, she had to conclude, were her fault. She might not have pushed Linn off the roof or even written about it happening, but she'd created the situation that drove Linn to be there in the first place. She might not have known she was doing it, but ignorance didn't seem like an adequate excuse for causing real people pain.

Latisha hadn't been planning on revealing to any of the crew where she was from and what she'd done in her old life, since she'd been sure they'd think she was insane. But now she knew for a fact that she couldn't say anything. They might accept her presence on the *Rake* now, but if they learned she was responsible for all their past and present predicaments, she was pretty sure that would change.

Chapter 8

Rodrigo knew it was going to be a terrible day the moment he stepped out of his cabin to see Grammy waiting for him, arms folded and expression grim.

Usually, if someone on the crew needed to talk to him about something, they'd wait until he made it to the galley and gotten some coffee before seeking him out. The only reason to catch him as soon as he was up was if something was very wrong indeed.

Sure enough, her first words to him were, "There's a situation that's come up. With Linn."

A jolt of alarm shot through him. "What's happened to her?" His imagination was all too good at supplying horrible scenarios, but he couldn't think of anything that could have happened to her since he saw her the evening before. If consequences from a past heist had caught up to them, then they would *all* be in trouble, not just Linn, so that couldn't be it.

"She's sprained her ankle," Grammy said tersely.

Relief filled him, and then confusion. Linn wasn't that accident-prone. He'd seen her scale rigging and duel men on a peaked roof without stumbling. And they hadn't even been up to anything dangerous in the past several hours.

"She tripped on the ladder going below and landed badly."

Rodrigo looked slowly from the ladder in question, barely six feet away, and back to Grammy. "Why didn't I hear anything?" He should've heard her fall, if it was bad enough to injure her—he might sleep late, but not that heavily. If nothing else, the resulting commotion should have roused him.

"She was trying to keep it quiet so you wouldn't find out. Thinks you'll get yourself in over your head without her along on this coming job." Grammy's tone clearly indicated that she shared this sentiment. "But regardless of what she might think, she's not going to be up for so much as a sedate minuet, let alone any derring-do, for at least a few weeks."

Under normal circumstances, Rodrigo flattered himself that he was adept at processing things rapidly and thinking on his feet. But now, he found himself freezing up, because this just didn't compute. Linn didn't get injured. *He* had been shot or stabbed a few times over the course of their career, but no one else on the crew had suffered more than some cuts and bruises since falling in with him.

An injury that would keep one of them from working for an extended period of time was unprecedented, and one that they picked up through simple everyday clumsiness was completely unthinkable.

A small, unpleasant voice in the back of his mind quietly queried *What other disasters could befall your crew that you didn't think were possible?*

"How's Asad?" he finally thought to ask. The two of them had had interesting times in the past, when it came to Linn, but maybe the navigator would share his feeling of having the rug pulled out from under him.

"Little bit shaken. I sent him and Ellis to get more horse chestnut for treating the sprain. They should be back soon." Grammy looked at him thoughtfully. "You've got that shindig at Lady Jennifer's in a few days, don't you?"

"I'll have to cancel," Rodrigo muttered. "Except—no, I can't. Blast." He'd been planning this heist with a very specific timing— he needed to maneuver his way into Lady Jennifer's affections by May Day, which was the biggest event on the Bartram Hall social calendar, and the perfect chaotic cover for some heirloom thievery.

Mysteriously skipping out on this invitation on such short notice would do nothing to increase her trust, and would, instead, likely damage it. But aside from Linn's notions that he needed watching, the final heist would be more likely to succeed if he had a partner, which meant that he needed to establish himself as someone with a plus-one.

"Thank you for telling me. I think I'd better discuss the situation with her," he concluded, before sidling past Grammy and ducking into Linn and Asad's cabin.

"I can't believe I was so stupid," Linn seethed, for at least the third time in their conversation.

"I'm just glad you're all right. Or going to be," Rodrigo reiterated. There weren't any chairs in the cabin, and he wasn't going to sit on the bed (because one of the sources of the current peace he and Asad had achieved was the establishment of certain boundaries), so he'd opted to sit on the floor instead of standing around. "But if we could consider that established, we still need to deal with the situation of the ball taking place in three days."

"You can't team up with Floriane Bonheur again," Linn said immediately.

Rodrigo blinked in surprise, reflexively bringing one hand to rest over the scar on his side. "Why would you think I'd so much as enter the same room as that woman again, let alone work with her?"

"You've made more questionable choices."

"I'll admit I've given second chances in the past to people who've swindled, betrayed, or tried to kill me, but never anyone who's gone three for three." Rodrigo sighed and scratched a hand through his hair. "I'm going to have to hire someone, aren't I."

"That's only a temporary solution," Linn pointed out, shifting to sit up on the bed a little more. "Whoever you take is going to have to be your partner for all the other stages of the job. If you hire a pretty face, you'll be stuck with dead weight later on, and if you get someone who knows what they're doing, odds are higher that they'll turn on you. Not to mention we can't afford it."

Both of them fell silent for a long, contemplative moment. Then, as if something had been jogged in his mind—maybe the mention of their finances, maybe something Grammy had said in the hall— he said slowly, "What about Ellis?"

Linn frowned, but not the way she did when she disagreed— more like the way she did when she found an idea intriguing and needed to pick at it for flaws. "Does she have the skill set? We don't know all that much about what she did before she was here."

"I think she'll do all right with the society part of it," Rodrigo said thoughtfully. "As for the less legal aspects, that can be taught. We've got several weeks before she would need to do much more than look polished and pretty. And, let's face it, she's about the only option we've got. The only people I trust completely are on this crew, and she and you are the only women of the right age here."

"There is the slight issue of her having avoided you like the plague since she arrived," Linn pointed out.

He shrugged. "I'll just have to be persuasive."

Rodrigo knew that Ellis knew he was watching her. She'd been stealing wary little glances at him all through dinner, almost like she thought he was a bomb about to go off. No one else seemed to notice—the whole crew was on edge, and had been all day, ever since it had become known that Linn was out of commission.

The tension had almost everyone scattering as soon as they'd finished their food. Asad lingered just long enough to help Linn limp back to their cabin, shooing Ruby, who seemed to have gotten the idea that she could eavesdrop if she pretended to be absorbed in her paperback, along as well.

Grammy and Ellis had only stuck around to clean up the dishes, but Rodrigo caught Ellis' arm as she made to follow the older woman with a stack of plates.

She visibly twitched when he touched her, but didn't try to pull away.

"There something you want from me, Captain?" she asked, voice even. "You've been staring at me all evening. It's getting creepy."

"I apologize if I disturbed you, but I need your assistance with a particular task."

"And what would that be." It sounded less like a question and more like a required line in a script.

"I don't know how much you know about how we make a living here—" he began.

"I've gotten a fair idea," Ellis cut in.

"Well, then, that makes this simpler. I need a partner for the job we have coming up, and for while I'm laying the groundwork. Linn would usually do this, but she won't be fully mobile until it's too late. So, I need you to take her place. You'd start by attending a ball with me three days from now, and we would train you in the other skills you'd need going forward."

A long silence hung between them, and finally Ellis asked, "What makes you assume I can dance?"

"You said you grew up middle-class," Rodrigo pointed out. "If you can't at least get through a quadrille and a waltz, I'd be very surprised. And you clearly have the manners to make it through a night in high society. It's in the way you talk and move and eat. Anything that you can't manage, I'll cover for you."

She still looked reluctant, almost like she was trying to find an excuse to say no but couldn't come up with one. "It should be fun, at least to begin with," he added. "Linn can lend you a gown from her stock, you'll get better food than you would here, and you can experience a bit of adventure." It was as close as he could come to "Why exactly are you so skittish about this? Because I don't think it's the lawbreaking and potential peril, I think it's me, and I don't understand."

But Ellis seemed to be doing the same mental calculations he and Linn had been doing earlier, and finally she said, "All right. I'll do it, since it doesn't seem like there's any other option." Her spine straightened slightly. "What do I have to do to get ready?"

Chapter 9

Latisha wasn't sure what had possessed her to agree to attend a ball with Rodrigo. The man was a menace to the female half of the species, and yet here she was, signing up to play his Disagreeable Fiancée for hours on end, and for more than one event, at that.

She was going to have to mingle with the snobbish upper crust that had always been her least favorite part of those awful books. She was going to, eventually, directly aid in the commission of a crime, something she had resigned herself to, as there didn't seem to be much point hoping that she would vanish back home before the heist rolled around.

But the fact remained that, now that she knew just how dire the crew's financial straits were, and now that she'd actually befriended them to some extent, she couldn't help but need to be part of the solution, rather than part of the problem. With Linn out of commission, the heist was the only way they were going to pull in any income for some time, and everything had to go perfectly.

Which meant that Rodrigo needed backup.

As long as she was here, she might as well put her inside knowledge to good use by helping out and pulling her weight. If she had wanted to be squeamish about criminal activity, she shouldn't have written a series about serial burglars and then moved in with said burglars. So, dressing up, mingling, and aiding and abetting it was.

Getting ready for the ball was, for the most part, easier than

Latisha had expected. Clothes were not an issue—Linn already had a few dresses for such occasions, and the gold-colored one Latisha picked only needed to be altered a little, mostly because Linn was a few inches taller. Reassuringly, the alterations were all tacked in place with stitches that would come out easily, which she took as a sign that she wasn't going to be stuck doing this forever. Linn would be back to her usual role as Rodrigo's right hand by the next heist, hopefully.

Perhaps it should have been a little alarming to be thinking that far ahead, but if it was, Latisha was too busy to take notice of it. She had roughly seventy-two hours to help Grammy fix the dress, hunt down cosmetics with Ruby since Linn's were too light for her complexion, rack her brains for anything she remembered from the ballroom dance classes she'd taken for "research", and go over protocol with Linn—both normal social things and tips for how to keep Rodrigo out of trouble.

Finally, and all too soon, the evening arrived. The gown, miraculously, turned out to be both comfortable and easy to maneuver in, although perhaps that was not so surprising, given what Linn usually got up to in it. It was also, Latisha had to admit quietly to herself, a gorgeous garment, as if the dress from *Beauty and the Beast* had acquired an extravagant bustle and met an eccentric clockwork enthusiast. With some experimentation, she was able to pull off a hairstyle that didn't make her want to cringe when she looked at herself ("artfully loose and carefree" was a very fine line to walk with curls like hers that had minds of their own).

She was reasonably sure she wouldn't make a fool of herself. The only problem remaining was coping with Rodrigo.

In stockinged feet and carrying her shoes, she made her way up to the deck, only to be hit with—

The setting sun had brushed over the ship and, like Midas, turned it to shades of gold. Rodrigo was silhouetted against its dying light. He turned as he heard her approach, and when he crossed to her, she could just make out the details of his features — the glossy raven hair that tumbled loose over his shoulders, his dark eyes widening slightly as he took her in, the sharp, clean lines of his jaw and cheekbones, the roguish smirk of his lips —

Latisha mentally slapped herself. Letting her turgid-prose voice kick in the first time she ever saw him was one thing, but this was completely uncalled-for. He was, all right, reasonably pretty to look at, but there were lots of good-looking men out there, especially in this world.

The suit he was wearing was admittedly a nice suit, with the waistcoat and cravat in dark greens that would complement her color scheme and match Lady Jennifer's and a jacket sprinkled with little ornamental gears, but the man himself had no particular right to make her pulse flutter.

And she didn't even like him, in any sense whatsoever. They had a job to do, and they needed to get it over with, hopefully without him deciding to do something as ridiculous as being attracted to her (or her to him).

Latisha was well aware of the potential tropes at play here, and she'd be on her guard to avoid them.

Rodrigo offered his arm. "Miss Ellis, will you do me the honor of accompanying me?"

Latisha took a deep breath, slipped into the role, and curtsied carefully. "Captain Antúnez, it would be my pleasure."

"Ah, that's Señor del Rey for tonight, though," Rodrigo corrected her with a smile.

Of course. Latisha had forgotten about his penchant for fake names on these schemes. She'd been starting to run out of new ones before she'd ended up here. This time around, he'd adopted the identity of Señor Antonio del Rey, a merchant from abroad who was settling down in the area.

Since this was Latisha's first time out, she hadn't been required to assume a fake name, to her relief. One false identity at a time was quite enough.

"Señor del Rey, then," she said, taking his arm as he led her towards the ship's railing. They'd briefly moored the Rake at a public skydock, one whose proprietors, for the right price, would remain blissfully ignorant of pesky things like legality. Towering steel girders elevated the expansive clapboard platform high enough off the ground to attract clientele and escape the purview of the law. Morality aside, this meant that Latisha wouldn't have to navigate a rope ladder in her dress. They could also arrive at and depart from the ball in a hired clock carriage, meaning that hopefully nobody would guess that they hadn't come from a townhouse like everyone else.

On the ground, rattling through the streets behind mechanical "horses" that only looked vaguely equine, Latisha couldn't help but stare out the window at the passing city. She hadn't had the presence of mind to get a very good look at things last time she was down here, beyond confirming that yes, she was in the last place she wanted to be.

Now she was struck more than ever by how right everything looked. She'd never done much description of the cities Rodrigo and the crew frequented beyond the basic map-layouts constructed for chase scenes. At least, not in a long time, not since everything had gone wrong.

But now that she was paying attention, the city seemed to have sprung straight out of her long-ago daydreams, when she'd been writing a story she loved instead of one she could sell.

Closer to the docks, their surroundings were clearly recognizable as an old-fashioned industrial park, with warehouses on every side. They passed through a neighborhood similar to the one where Monachus' shop was located, and from there into progressively more affluent areas, discernible by the increasing size of the houses and the lots they were built on, and by the ever more extravagant architecture that marked the homes of the grandfolk.

And then they arrived, and there was no time to ponder

anymore.

Bartram Hall wasn't quite the most elaborate house Latisha had spotted, but it was close. Large portions of the exterior featured curving walls made of clear glass panes, revealing the guests milling inside. Sculpted copper tendrils as thick as a man's waist, allowed to turn green with verdigris, rambled over the whole structure, looking like either vines or tentacles.

Rodrigo helped her out of the clock carriage and guided her up the front steps as she tried to take everything in at once. In a blur, Latisha went through the motions of handing over her wrap and a card, following Rodrigo through a series of hallways and up a staircase all in shades of green—she was irritated to realize that he now seemed like the most reliable thing in this stunningly perilous environment—and entering a spacious ballroom that blazed with light and was packed with dark-suited men and women in jewel-toned gowns.

Rodrigo guided them towards the tables of food and drink off to one side as soon as they'd been announced, a move that Latisha initially thought was to give her a moment. Their path crossed, however, with a strikingly red-haired young woman in an emerald-green gown, and Latisha, recognizing her, realized the opposite was true.

They were jumping into this right off the bat.

"Good evening, Lady Jennifer," Rodrigo said smoothly, bowing low and kissing the woman's proffered hand. Latisha curtsied just in time and did her best to look disgusted with him. It wasn't difficult.

"We meet again, Señor del Rey," Lady Jennifer replied. Latisha would have recognized her even without the name. She'd already started thinking about how to describe that very dress for the first ball. There was something about the eyes that bothered her, though. She couldn't put her finger on it. "I am so pleased you were able to attend. And who might this be?"

"Ah, yes. Lady Jennifer, allow me to present my fiancée." He tinged the word with a touch of disdain. "Miss Amora Ellis. Miss Ellis, Lady Jennifer Bartram."

"Pleased to meet you, my lady," Latisha managed. "I cannot thank you enough for your kind invitation."

"Oh, you mustn't mention it," Lady Jennifer said lightly. "After all, Señor del Rey was quite gallant, coming to my rescue a few weeks ago when my carriage horses decided to run away with me. And then the other day, when he swept me out of harm's way before that mysteriously broken shop sign could fall on me."

A flash of amusement crossed Lady Jennifer's face, and Latisha suddenly realized what it was that bothered her about the woman's green eyes. They were intelligent, seeing right through Rodrigo's ridiculously convoluted contrivances to flirt with her.

Latisha had written all sorts of heroines for Rodrigo to steal from, but the one thing none of them had ever been was clever. And Lady Jennifer was.

She was on to Rodrigo, yet invited him to her ball anyway— why? To see what he would do? To toy with him? Whatever the reason, Latisha needed to talk with the captain about this as soon as they were well away. There was no way he was prepared to deal with a target who actually had a brain.

"I should let you dance with your . . . fiancée," Lady Jennifer was saying, "but I hope our paths will cross again before the night is over." And she swept away.

Once she was gone, Rodrigo turned to Latisha. "Are you all right?"

"I'll be fine. She was just . . . different than I'd expected," Latisha said hesitantly. "Didn't she seem, I don't know, a little off to you? Like she was having a joke at our expense."

Rodrigo frowned and shook his head. "Not especially. No more than any of the grandfolk I've met. Why?"

Latisha tried to think of a way to explain without mentioning their real purpose here or her own secrets, and failed. "Never mind. Now what happens?"

"Now we dance. When I tell you, we'll pull off to one side and stage a quarrel, then part ways in a huff. I'll make my way to Lady Jennifer and bemoan my sorry lot in life, and you'll slip out and explore the house. The May Day Ball should also take place here, so anything you can find that would be useful for planning purposes will help."

Latisha nodded. "I can manage that."

"I know you can," Rodrigo said warmly, so much so that it startled her. "Now come on."

He took her hand and moved out onto the floor as a new set started. Latisha had had three days to mentally prepare for dancing with Rodrigo and discovered that that still hadn't been enough, because none of her expectations turned out to be accurate.

She'd assumed he would be flamboyant and controlling, sweeping her across the floor with excessive passion, pressing her so close to him that she would feel his breath. But instead, he let her keep a little distance within a proper waltz frame, and moved with a quiet, liquid grace, guiding her with the subtlest of pressures on her hand or the small of her back.

Somehow, ridiculously, this made it more difficult to keep her composure, and she was acutely aware that she was as stiff as a board, an unhelpful contrast to his easy maneuvering.

At long last—maybe not even an hour later, though it felt like a much longer span of time—Rodrigo began to maneuver them more to the edge of the dance floor, towards a relatively out-of-the-way alcove. Leaning close, he murmured in her ear, "Now would be a good time to start staging that argument."

"What do I argue with you about?" Latisha would never have imagined saying that to Rodrigo, if she'd ever imagined meeting him at all, but most of the things she would have wanted to pick a fight with him about were things that would probably expose her as knowing more than she should.

And this evening, astonishingly, he hadn't done anything to

deserve her getting angry with him.

"Anything you like. It doesn't even have to be a real argument as long as we keep it quiet enough. Just make it look like it is and say whatever you like."

Like *Singing in the Rain*, Latisha thought, but that wasn't much help either. They hadn't really talked all evening, and she wasn't sure where to begin. Finally, in desperation, she asked "Why did you start doing this?"

Rodrigo, to his credit, played right along. "Doing what?"

"The heists." They'd made it to the alcove; Latisha yanked her hand out of Rodrigo's and planted her fists on her hips. "Of all the infinite varieties of a life of crime you could've picked, why something as complicated and risky as romancing your way into rich women's jewel safes?"

He blinked, looking taken aback. She wasn't sure if it was a genuine response or part of the pantomime. "I . . . I don't know. I did it once, and we pulled it off and made a lot of money, so I suppose we just kept on."

Latisha wanted to push him further, get better answers, but reminded herself that she already knew what the truth was. He'd started the heists and carried on with them because that was what she had written. Instead, she let out a frustrated huff, shot him a parting look of scorn, and turned on her heel to flounce away. Or, at least, what she hoped was something akin to flouncing. She'd never been quite sure what that was meant to look like.

Quit poking at problems you can't understand or solve, she told herself sharply. *Just do what you need to do to survive here, and quit worrying about something as ridiculous as Rodrigo's feelings.*

Now there was something she'd never expected to have to say.

Chapter 10

Rodrigo was experiencing a problem. That wasn't necessarily unusual, but the particular issue at hand was. He could see Lady Jennifer approaching, knew she would reach him in moments—and he had no idea what he was going to say to her.

Well, perhaps that wasn't quite true—he did have a few ideas for how to begin—but normally he *knew* beyond a doubt what would be the right thing to say to a mark. He never had to think about it; the words would just float to the surface in his mind and roll off his tongue and everything would fall into place. It had bothered him sometimes in the past, even frightened him a little, but it was undeniably useful.

Only now Lady Jennifer was four, three, two steps away, and the *words weren't coming*.

He spared the briefest of moments to wish that he could have continued spending the evening with Ellis, maybe even that they hadn't been here for crime and could have just done what they pleased. He still couldn't figure out why she disliked him, but he liked to think that they'd come a little closer to her being comfortable with him over the course of the evening. They were going to need to work on the way she danced, though . . .

"Has the lovely Miss Ellis abandoned you?" Lady Jennifer inquired, eyebrow arched as she joined him in the alcove.

You've got a brain. Use it. "Alas, she has," Rodrigo confirmed mournfully. "We quarreled rather badly. Well, to tell the truth, the quarrel never seems to end these days, only pause for a moment here and there."

"And what did you do to provoke her wrath this time?"

He produced a small huff of bitter laughter. "You say that as if I had some way to tell. No, it's taken me some time, and more than my share of grief and guilt, but I've finally concluded that her moods will do what they will irrespective of my actions. I can no more claim responsibility for her fits of anger than I can for the changing of the winds."

Lady Jennifer tilted her head, considering him. "Then you must be less of a gentleman than I thought you, Señor del Rey, for I have always believed that it is a gentleman's place to take full responsibility for his lady's happiness and well-being. If he does not know the things that will disrupt them, he is simply not paying enough attention."

Blast, no, she was supposed to be sympathizing with him at this point. Why wasn't she sympathizing?

Silently apologizing to Ellis for the slander he was about to unload on her alias, Rodrigo threw up his hands in staged exasperation. "Believe me, my lady, I have tried to learn what will anger her—have been trying for our entire courtship. But there is simply no consistency from which a man may learn. If I compliment her appearance, I am in danger of being labeled a lecher. If I ask her how she has been since I last saw her, I will like as not be accused of being controlling and giving her no privacy. If I speak of my business, I am boastful and self-centered. If I do not speak to her at all, I am an uncaring cad. On this occasion, I merely commented on the number of other couples in attendance, by way of innocent observation, and she became convinced that I was paying some other woman more attention than her."

Both of Lady Jennifer's eyebrows were raised now. "Then, if you will not consider it impolite, I must ask: assuming you are innocent of all these accusations, why remain engaged to a lady who so abuses you?"

He couldn't tell whether she was actually curious or trying to poke holes in his story and did his best to not shiver under the gaze of her bright green eyes. "Not because I wish it, I can assure you. Our relationship sprung from an . . . arrangement with her father, before I ever met the lady, and I have been trapped in it ever since." He turned his eyes to the polished floor. "Tonight, though, she may not have been the only one in the wrong—I must confess my attention did stray to a certain other lady here, more than once."

Please be sympathetic, please be sympathetic, he thought desperately. He wasn't completely sure what he was doing, but he was quite sure that getting into an argument about the principles of fidelity when applied to a shrewish fiancée would not help him.

"Indeed. How scandalous." Lady Jennifer's tone was just enough on this side of teasing to keep him from losing all hope. "I should inform you that the severity of my judgment for your error will depend entirely on the other lady in question; tell me who it was at once."

Rodrigo had learned years ago how to make his face redden in faux embarrassment, and he did so now. "If you must know, my lady," he said, still avoiding eye contact with anything more than a foot above the floor, "the one who caught my attention so irresistibly . . . was yourself."

He finally flicked his gaze up to meet hers, his whole body taut with the nerves of the moment. Everything hinged on her receptiveness to his "confession" (not entirely false—he had been keeping an eye on her), and he had no way of knowing whether the words he'd just uttered were the right ones, or the ones that would doom the whole heist before it began.

She smiled, slow and victorious, like she'd caught him at something. "In that case, you are entirely forgiven, and you may ask me to dance."

Relief surged through him, threatening to leave him leaning limp against the wall if his control had been any less refined. "In that case, my lady," he said, painting his expression in beatific delight and extending a hand, "may I have the honor of this dance?"

"You may." Lady Jennifer placed her hand lightly in his.

He bowed, and the music for the new set started at precisely the right moment as he led her out onto the floor.

Some half-dozen sets later, as he was bringing Lady Jennifer out of a particularly glamorous dip, Rodrigo finally spotted Ellis slipping back into the ballroom, scanning this way and that as if looking for him.

When she finally did spot him, she didn't give the "disaster has struck, drop everything and let's go" signal that he'd taught her, but he decided he didn't care. The past hour of dancing and flirtatious small talk would have to do.

He was mentally exhausted from trying to lay on the charm without the usual safety net in his mind and starting to get physically worn out as well—Lady Jennifer was not one of the more sedate partners he'd ever shared a dance floor with.

So as the music ended, he bowed and said, "I'm afraid, my lady, that I must take my leave—my fiancée has just returned, and I fear if I do not depart with her immediately, she may cause a scene."

"We mustn't have that," Lady Jennifer agreed, inclining her head. "Farewell then for tonight, Señor del Rey. I wish you the best of luck with your turbulent engagement."

"A wish unlikely to be granted, but I admire your hope." Rodrigo bent and kissed her gloved hand. "Until we meet again, my lady, and—if I may be so bold—I pray it may be soon."

He didn't quite bolt then—he was Captain Rodrigo Antúnez, and he did not flee from a mark—but he did turn on his heel with perhaps a tad more haste than strictly necessary, and swiftly cross the ballroom to where Ellis was waiting.

She was well into character when he reached her, arms folded and an expression of betrayed rage on her face, but she flinched ever so slightly when he slipped his arm through hers to pull her away from the gathering. She hadn't seemed to mind his touch earlier, even if she hadn't been entirely comfortable, so he wasn't sure what might be different now.

That, he decided, was something that needed to be investigated before they dealt with anything else, so once they'd made their way out of the house and bundled themselves into a passing clock-carriage, he turned to her and asked firmly, "Ellis, are you afraid of me?"

"What? No." But she wouldn't meet his eyes. "Why would I be afraid of you?"

"I haven't a clue. I've been trying to figure it out, but I haven't been able to come up with anything plausible. You're comfortable with everyone else on the crew, even Asad, and yet you avoid me whenever you can and you're clearly uncomfortable with me touching you. Whatever it is, you won't be in trouble and I'll do my best to understand. We have to be able to work together and trust each other to pull this heist off, and right now something's preventing that for you. So please, tell me so we can work around it."

Ellis' face went flush with embarrassment. "It's nothing. It's ridiculous, I can handle it myself."

Rodrigo was not going to be so easily swayed. "I need to know, Ellis."

She stared at her folded hands in their gold silk gloves. "It's just . . . you do know you have a reputation, right? For, for seducing women and breaking their hearts."

He wasn't sure how to answer that. He was more or less aware that word of his past heists had gotten around, which was why he used the aliases. But he'd mostly thought of that in terms of being known as a wanted criminal, rather than as some kind of womanizing urban legend.

Fortunately, Ellis went on without him actually needing to answer. "I'd heard of you and what you did before I met you and realized who you were. And I mean, it might be blown out of proportion, like a lot of gossip is, but the general consensus is that you must be doing something to make so many women just melt all over you and let you get away with stealing their most valuable jewelry right under their noses." She clenched her hands, hard enough that the fabric started to wrinkle. "There's a lot who think that if a woman just gets too close to you, or talks to you or touches you too much, she'll, I don't know, fall hopelessly in love with you for no reason." She laughed nervously. "It's ridiculous, but so many ridiculous things are true these days that I was . . . wary, I suppose."

Rodrigo couldn't quite find words for a moment, and when he could, the first thing out of his mouth was, "Linn's been living and working with me for years, and she's never been in love with me. She's married to someone else."

Ellis' mouth might have twisted wryly there for a moment, but he couldn't be certain in the dimly lit carriage. "There are some rumors that she is, though. That she's cheating on Asad with you, or—but anyway, I could tell right away that that wasn't true. Which was part of why I figured it'd be safe to agree to do this in the first place. I suppose I'm still just a bit . . . on edge."

Rodrigo frowned, reaching carefully for one of her hands. She let him take it. "I won't deny that a certain amount of charm and charisma are tools that I regularly use on these jobs," he began, "but I never set out to make someone so attached to me that they would break their heart over me." It did seem to happen with disturbing regularity without him trying, but since he didn't know how to explain that, any more than he could explain the force that kept driving him back to heists of this nature, he didn't bring it up. "And I only use those tools on someone whose excessive valuables I'm trying to purloin. Never on my crew. You and the others have my respect and are treated accordingly."

Mercifully, Ellis seemed to relax slightly at that. He squeezed her hand gently and let it go. "We'll work on that trust. I want you to feel safe with me, Ellis. With all of us."

She nodded. "Um . . . and did you want to hear what I found out about the house, while you were with Lady Jennifer?"

"Very much. How far were you able to explore, and do you think anyone spotted you?"

Ellis shook her head and went on to outline a surprisingly detailed layout of the townhouse, complete with useful nooks to duck out of the path of any passing servants and even some details on Lady Jennifer's bedchamber. "I wasn't able to find the safe, though," she added at the end.

"No need to worry. We'll have some other chances to snoop around." Rodrigo couldn't keep an impressed grin from spreading onto his face. "That's already far more than I expected you to get your first time out. We'll make a solid criminal of you yet."

She just ducked her head again, like she wasn't sure whether to take that as a compliment or not. "It wasn't all that difficult. It . . . felt familiar, somehow."

"Then you must have a good sense for these things—if you're not careful, I might have to always take you as my second on these jobs." He was only partially teasing.

"Don't push your luck, Captain." But she was almost smiling as she said it, so Rodrigo counted it as a success.

Chapter 11

There had been a note on her pillow when Latisha had come in during the small hours of the night, informing her in Grammy's scratchy scrawl that she had earned a day off from the galley and could sleep in as late as she liked.

Latisha, therefore, had no compunctions about only waking up in the late morning. She took her time getting up and dressed and made her way to the galley in a leisurely fashion to see if there was any breakfast left. She was fairly sure there would be—Rodrigo tended to sleep late even when he hadn't been out half the night, and there always seemed to be food around for him.

She wasn't sure what she would do when she inevitably ran into him, or how she would be around him going forward. She was slowly starting to accept that he might not be the despicable person she'd made him out to be, and she'd gotten a slightly better idea of how he thought and operated during their conversation last night (as well as ascertaining that the fan fiction she knew about wasn't true), but . . . something still bothered her. Something she couldn't put her finger on.

She was still pondering the issue as she left the galley a few minutes later, no leftovers to be found. At that point, she ran out of time to think about it, because Rodrigo himself scrambled down the ladder from the deck, looking far more bright-eyed and energetic than she would've expected given the hour.

"Good, you're up. I need you with me for something," he said.

Latisha blinked at him in confusion. "What are we doing?"

"A trust-building exercise."

The completely ridiculous mental image of doing trust falls with him or untangling herself from a human knot with the crew sprang into her mind, but she had the feeling he meant something else entirely.

"I sent Ruby to pay another few hours' docking fees, since you said you'd never gone high before you took up with us. We're overdue on introducing you to some elements of skydweller culture. So come on, we're going to the Bairn and Sparrowhawk."

Even after taking a moment to rack her brain, Latisha was fairly sure she'd never written any such place into this world. She was almost certain, in fact, that she'd never built any kind of "skydweller culture" into the *Rakish Heart* novels at all.

Except . . . oh, she had, long ago and far away, when she'd drafted Rodrigo and Linn's first adventure as a stand-alone story rather than the first of too many serial romances. She'd forgotten a lot of the details over the ensuing years, but clearly, they had still stuck around.

She'd never actually contradicted most of that worldbuilding, after all, and instead had just left it to molder in an unpublished manuscript.

Only now, she had the chance to actually see it.

"All right, then," she said, coming down the hall to join him, "but what's the Bairn and Sparrowhawk?"

She said it with a lot more eagerness than she'd displayed for pretty much anything since arriving.

Rodrigo seemed a little taken aback by it, but didn't let it throw him. "It's a pub, of course. Most skydocks have one, especially if they cater to people like us. A lot of skydwellers don't like to spend too much time on the ground when they're not on a job—too much risk of getting nabbed—but staying on shipboard too long with just your crew is a recipe for bickering and grudges and all kinds of unpleasantness. The skydocks offer some space to get away and stretch our legs, and they're at high enough altitude that the law won't bother anyone. So, they tend to have businesses spring up that cater to that. The Bairn's among the most popular, though — there should be a good crowd there today. Lots of people who just got paid."

He led her across the deck and onto the docks as he spoke. Now that she wasn't distracted by an impending infiltration and trying not to form an opinion about how well Rodrigo wore a suit, Latisha was better able to take in everything around her.

She'd noticed the open square of buildings between the docking area and the stairwell at the center of the platform but had assumed they were warehouses or some kind of administrative buildings. Instead, if the signage was accurate, they appeared to include a hostel, a pawnshop that seemed to mostly buy and sell weaponry, a general store, and the pub that Rodrigo was steering her towards. It must have been the place he had described, as it had a surprisingly well-painted sign of an infant riding a bird of prey over the door.

Rodrigo shot her a reassuring grin and held the door open for her.

A wave of sound and scent and color washed over Latisha, nearly sweeping her off her feet, but in the best of ways. She couldn't look at everything enough.

She hadn't written this place, with its aeronautical paraphernalia ornamenting the board walls, the customers slouched at tables or perched along the bar in their mismatched, gear-festooned attire, the casual way everyone wore their assortments of outlandish guns and blades like they would a jacket, the relaxed cacophony of talking and laughter and swearing, and the smell of smoke and spilled drink and some *truly* amazing stew.

But it was precisely the kind of place she would have daydreamed of back in those early days — someplace she would have tried to use as a setting, maybe for Linn and Rodrigo to go relax after a long day. It was like a tiny slice of her world as she'd once believed it could be, rather than what she'd turned it into.

The delight welling up inside her must have shown on her face, because Rodrigo's smile had turned slightly startled. "You haven't been here before, have you, Ellis?" he inquired. "You look like you just came home."

Latisha managed a shrug, only slightly saddened by her need to perpetuate the lie. "I . . . I suppose I never realized that anywhere like this actually existed," she half-explained. "Also, I don't know what food I'm smelling, but I need some."

That made him chuckle. "You might have to fight for it— Anthea's stew tends to bring that out in people." Hand on her elbow, he nudged their way through the chaos of bodies until they were closer to the bar. "Anthea! Got a new crew member getting her aether-baptism—we're going to need stew and a round of drinks."

A woman, maybe in her early forties, with wild brown curls escaping a green scarf that clashed brilliantly with her violet dress, sauntered over to them and gave Latisha an assessing look. "Thought you were done taking in strays, Roddy."

Rodrigo threw up his hands in mock helplessness. "So did I. But you'd think I'd know better than to make any kind of plans like that by now, wouldn't you?"

"Just as long as you plan to pay your tab on time." Anthea's mouth quirked in a half-smile aimed at Latisha. "Mind yourself with this one, honey. No denying he's a gentleman, but more often than not he's broke, and I've lost count of how many times he's made some excuse about having to pay me later."

"Slander and lies," Rodrigo shot back smoothly. "I happen to have coin with me, enough for today if not enough to close out the tab."

Anthea's eyebrows went up, but she fetched the stew and a couple of dark bottles of ale. When Rodrigo produced a few coins to cover it, she muttered "I guess Hafidi let you have your allowance," but took the money all the same.

Their luck held out long enough to furnish them with empty seats in a corner where Latisha could continue to drink everything in and devour the stew. It was, if anything, even better than it smelled. She had nearly finished it and was starting to think that maybe this extended trip down the rabbit hole actually had some pleasant things to offer, when a band of some sort that had been setting themselves up on the tiny dais in the corner started to play.

People started to push tables and chairs back to make space to dance. Given the opportunity, she might have enjoyed the chance to watch, but before she could think that far, Rodrigo's hand appeared in her peripheral vision.

"Dance with me, Ellis?" he inquired, voice raised to be heard over the mix of fiddle, flute, concertina, and unknown strumming instrument that was filling up the room.

"I thought we covered that last night," was all she could think to say.

"Yes, and you were stiff and nervous the whole time. Come on, this is the trust-building part."

"I don't know how to dance to this."

"Neither do half these idiots. I'll show you." And with that, he caught hold of her hand and pulled her to her feet, leading her out into the cleared space. "Just hold onto me like if we were waltzing, and mirror what I do with my feet."

The dance that he was pulling her into seemed, after a little observation and trial and error, to be a patchwork combination of a polka and a sailor's hornpipe, with elements Latisha thought she remembered from a flirtation with swing dancing thrown in for good measure. Keeping from falling and getting trampled necessitated her pressing herself a little closer to Rodrigo than she would've perhaps preferred, but she did have to appreciate the strength and grace in how he led her through the steps and turns.

Well, me mother used to tell me, back in a softer time, someone in the band began to sing,

"Keep on the straight and narrow, son. Don't live a life of crime."

But I couldn't keep from trouble, no matter how I'd try,
And that is why you find me here a-livin' in the sky.

The rest of the band—and some of the patrons, Latisha wasn't sure how the ones dancing could find breath—joined in on the chorus.

The law's mostly rot, the grandfolk the same,
The city is too narrow and the countryside too tame.
So, if you would do better, lads, then come away and fly—
You'll never find a better lot than livin' in the sky.

The song went on, with verses about stealing food to survive, kissing the Mayor's daughter, and kicking an irritating nobleman in the seat of the pants, but Latisha could barely keep track, since most of her attention was on not getting separated from Rodrigo or tripping him up.

With a jolt of surprise, she realized that she was actually having *fun*. The evening before, she'd been too caught up in the tension of the situation to find any enjoyment, but here and now, where everything around her was like something out of her best daydreams, it was different. All she had to do was move and not worry about secrets or heists or anything worse than accidentally smacking into someone nearby. And not even about that, really, because Rodrigo wasn't going to put her anywhere she wasn't supposed to be.

The music ended with a triumphant flourish, and he dipped her over one leg. She'd been busy enough keeping track of her feet that she'd forgotten how close he was, but now she abruptly remembered.

His face was only a few inches away from hers, his panting breath brushing her ear, and—

She tilted her head just so and kissed him, not caring how many other people were watching. All that mattered was the sharp, sweet sound as she stole his breath—

NO

Latisha blinked rapidly, then shook her head to try and clear away the unhelpful narration. Dancing was one thing, but she couldn't just spring a kiss on him, even if it momentarily seemed like a good idea.

Rodrigo pulled her upright, looking concerned. "Are you all right, Ellis?"

How was she supposed to answer that? "I'm fine. Just . . . " Perhaps the smartest thing would be to say she'd had enough of dancing, but she wasn't actually sure she wanted to stop or leave this place that had otherwise been untainted so far by what she'd turned her world into. "Just don't dip me like that again, I think."

"Fair enough." The band was starting up another tune. "Another dance, or would you rather sit?"

She took a deep breath. "I think the trust-building needs a little bit more work. Don't you?"

When they returned to the *Rake* some hours later, with the sun getting lower in the sky, Latisha half-expected to see Asad or Linn waiting for them on deck, anxious to get going. But although they were there, they were busy with their own tasks, and it was Grammy who watched her and Rodrigo as they boarded the ship.

"I see you spent your day off well," was all she said.

Under other circumstances, Latisha might've puzzled over this more, but her head was already spinning with everything else that had happened. Mostly what had her so distracted was trying to reevaluate Rodrigo.

Today, with her, he'd been more like she'd originally imagined him—a lovable rogue rather than a womanizing dandy. The more she thought about it, the more she concluded that he'd been like that ever since she arrived, really. She just hadn't been able to see it because she'd been looking for reasons to dislike him. Now she wasn't sure what to do.

After some additional thought, she decided to not worry about it for the moment. She'd had a wonderful day—brief moment of attraction to her protagonist/employer aside—and she might as well leave it at that. If this played out anything like the portal fantasy stories she remembered from her childhood, she'd probably be sent home once the heist was done, anyway, and then all this would become moot.

Chapter 12

Rodrigo was of the opinion that taking Ellis to the Bairn and Sparrowhawk had been one of the best decisions he'd made in a long time, and he thought it was definitely worth the coin he'd expended in the process.

Not only had she had a good time—that odd moment when he dipped her notwithstanding, especially since she hadn't had a problem when he'd attempted it at Lady Jennifer's, though perhaps he'd been telegraphing his intentions more then—but she'd been noticeably more relaxed around him ever since. There was still a certain wariness on occasion, but she no longer seemed to be wishing herself on the other side of the world whenever he came within ten feet of her.

Not that he had any clue why their little expedition had brought about such a change. The why didn't matter. What mattered was that he had had the feeling that it would work, and it had. Now Ellis' problem was solved, and he knew he could still trust his gut to some extent.

Linn, however, took a somewhat different view of the situation. A couple of days after, she pulled him aside with a muttered, "We need to talk," and shut them both in her cabin. She turned to face him, arms folded and an angry, brittle expression on her face.

Rodrigo hadn't seen her look like that in . . . years. Not since the very earliest days of their friendship.

"What is it?" he inquired.

She seemed to need a moment to find the words. "Look," she finally began, "I know there's a way that this works—a system that we have in place. You're the captain, you make the plans, and you go haring off doing stupid things while I keep everything held together and functioning. And that's fine, I've always been fine with that. But Rodrigo, that means that when I say our finances are falling down a hole, I really mean it and you *need* to listen to me instead of spending more than we can afford to go out drinking with a new hire."

"It wasn't that much—" Rodrigo began, even though he knew that wasn't quite the main point.

"That's what I'm trying to get at. *Anything*, right now, is more than we can afford. We're going to need to restock soon, and as of right now, there's things we'll have to do without because we're that broke." She sighed, looking additionally frazzled as she went on. "It would have been that way even without your escapade the other day, but that didn't help any."

Rodrigo blinked, lost for words. They'd been tight on money before—that had been the impetus for at least half of their heists—but it had never made Linn sound quite so desperate and despairing. "I'm . . . sorry. Why didn't you say something before it got this bad?"

"Because," Linn said tightly, "up until fairly recently, I was operating under the assumption that I could do something about the situation. But now I've got a bad ankle out of nowhere, and even once I'm better, Asad's going to be too nervous to back me up for a while."

"What are you talking about?"

She lifted her chin and looked him dead in the eye. "The only reason we've stayed solvent as long as we have is because Asad and I have been going out on burglary runs at least once a month, since before we were even married. I used to do it sometimes before he joined the crew, but not very often—it's easier with a partner. We steal what won't be missed, what we can easily fence.

That's made up the majority of our income for years now."

Rodrigo had to take a moment to process this. "Why didn't you say anything?" he finally asked. "I could have helped you, or maybe even stopped the heists and found something different."

Linn's laugh was short and bitter. "I tried to get you to stop the heists before, ages ago. Do you even remember? You certainly didn't seem to be paying any attention at the time."

"Things are different now, though." He hadn't been quite sure about this until he said it, but speaking the words seemed to make it more real. "Since Ellis came, I haven't felt trapped in this heist like I usually do. I . . . I really think I could stop." He thought back to the money he'd unthinkingly spent and winced. "I mean, we should probably finish this one and make a little coin to keep us going until you're healed up and we can figure out something else, but . . . I feel like I have a choice about it, and I didn't before."

Linn regarded him for a long moment, then sighed, letting her gaze drop. "Fine. If you really think you could end it—the sooner we can make the change, the better. You . . . haven't always been yourself, on the heists, and it scares me. Sometimes I've wondered if this was the time you'd be gone for good—if my friend was ever going to come back out of that swaggering shell."

Rodrigo stared at the floor, knowing he should make eye contact but not quite able to bring himself to do so. "We've been rough on each other," he admitted. "We don't talk, and when we do, it's always a fight about something. Usually something stupid I've done." A thought occurred to him, and he shot Linn a sharp look, clarifying, "Except for hiring Ellis. That was definitely a good decision, and you won't convince me otherwise."

Astonishingly, Linn laughed, and not in a bitter way at all. "I've already conceded that one. Just try and romance her with something that doesn't spend coin next time."

Once again, Rodrigo was lost for words. "I—that wasn't romancing her!" he eventually spluttered. "We needed to build trust. For the next infiltration, so she would look like she wanted to be there instead of like she'd been kidnapped."

Linn just smirked at him as she ducked out the cabin door. "You can call it that if you like," she fired back. "I'm all for you spending time around her—unlike some people, I'm not going to lurk jealously in a corner because my friend has finally found someone. Just don't break her heart and don't spend our fuel money."

So obviously, what started happening afterward was entirely Linn's fault. She'd put the idea into his head.

He definitely hadn't had any kind of amorous designs on Ellis before his first mate started insinuating things, and such feelings certainly weren't his motivation for offering to teach her some basic swordsmanship. He simply agreed with Linn's assessment that Ellis could stand to have some additional skills under her belt if she was going to be his second for this heist, and the ability to defend herself was a key component of that.

Not that she wasn't unmistakably lovely—she'd taken the breath out of him when he'd first seen her in that gold dress Linn lent her —but he'd encountered any number of breathtaking women and stolen from most of them. That wasn't relevant in any way to the situation at hand.

Having secured a few hours of Ellis' time from Grammy, he led her onto the deck and presented her with one of the less complex swords from the ship's weapons stock—a single, straight dueling blade with a plain hilt and scuffed leather sheath.

"Theoretically, you could conceal a knife in your dress or in one of your boots at a ball but given that you haven't really done any fighting before, you might prefer to fight with a weapon that lets you keep an opponent further away," he explained. "Or a gun would work, too, but if you're going to try shipboard target practice, it's better to have clear skies and open country so you can make sure you won't hit anyone."

Ellis was holding the sword by the sheath in both hands and looking at it dubiously, like it might bite her. "Okay, yeah, but that doesn't explain how I would sneak something like this into a formal event. Those skirts are pretty bulky, but not that bulky."

"There's always a few military men about the place wearing dueling swords or sabers like an accessory," Rodrigo shrugged. "They're not difficult to pilfer in a pinch—I'll teach you once you get the basics down."

"Still doesn't explain why you think that I'd need to use one of these. Or that I'd be any good at it."

"You've ended up mastering pretty much everything else you've been called upon to do around here. And as for the why . . . " Rodrigo smirked. "So that you can rescue me if I need it, of course."

This was perfectly true, but it was also intended to make her laugh and put her at ease. When this didn't happen, he gave it up and tried to edge into a more serious and instructor-ly tone as he had her unsheathe the sword. He worked with her on her grip, her stance, and a couple of basic moves.

Oddly enough, teaching her seemed to be what did relax her, and while she was still far from ready for actually engaging anyone by the time the session was over, she had made progress.

Grammy kept letting him borrow her every day thereafter, although after the third or fourth time she started giving him knowing looks that were quite uncalled for, thank you. Moreover, after a couple of weeks she'd somehow gotten the whole crew doing it.

What was the world coming to when you couldn't even train someone who needed it without everyone taking you for a lovestruck fool with ulterior motives?

Two and a half weeks in, Ellis had grasped enough of a variety of parries, slashes, and ripostes and picked up enough confidence to ask, "Are you ever going to spar with me? I just thought, I don't know, that was how these kinds of . . . training things worked."

It was a good idea, and Rodrigo couldn't deny that he hadn't had the opportunity for a good spar in some time, what with Linn being increasingly busy, irritable, and then injured. He ought to keep in practice, even if Ellis wasn't skilled enough yet to properly challenge him.

He grinned and fetched an extra sword from the weapons cupboard, finding her waiting with her guard up when he returned.

The mock duel, as he'd anticipated, didn't last terribly long. He left himself open at first, inviting her to attack him, but when she remained in her defensive stance—a wiser choice, anyway—he moved in, going on the offensive. He went easy on her, and she made up in determination some of what she lacked in experience, so the spar lasted a decent amount of time

Minutes later, he backed her into a corner. She tried to strike out, but he caught the hilt of her sword with his, pressing in close so she didn't have space to disentangle.

She tilted her head back to flash a smile at him. Then, instead of trying to back further away, she pushed forward.

Caught off guard, Rodrigo stumbled back, giving her room to escape, which she immediately tried to take advantage of.

He caught and disarmed her seconds later, just before Ruby came running up onto the deck to deliver the message that Grammy wanted Ellis' help with dinner and she should knock off playing around and go clean up.

Ellis was gone below deck shortly thereafter, with a cheerful, out-of-breath thanks for the lesson as usual, but Rodrigo, left to his own devices, found he couldn't get his mind away from that moment. The way Ellis had looked riding high on the rush of the sparring—like when they danced, only more purposeful somehow —that grin of premature triumph, how her flyaway curls had escaped to frame her face, how her breathless body felt so close to his . . .

He tried not to think about it, if only to avoid proving his entire smirking crew right, but he had almost no success. To make matters worse, he couldn't lie to himself about it anymore—Ellis was not only attractive in the general sense, but he, specifically, was attracted to her.

If he could have avoided her, it might have been easier, but he couldn't stop the daily dueling lessons without giving the reason why, and beyond that, Linn seemed bent on compounding his difficulties by announcing she was including Ellis in some of the planning for the heist.

"She's the one who's actually going to be there; it only makes sense," his conniving first mate pointed out.

Ellis agreed, probably because it was a good point, but now Rodrigo was contending with routinely having her sitting near him and reaching past him for notes and floor plans. Worse, her intelligence and strong will were now on full display, qualities that had always been his weakness and were not helping him mitigate how enamored he was becoming with her.

Not to mention the questions that he didn't know how to answer.

"Why do you wait for an invitation to a ball to run the heist when you could just slip in and out some evening and get what you need?" she asked one morning.

At the other end of the table, Asad fell into an inexplicable coughing fit, made all the more suspicious by the fact that he didn't technically need to breathe.

"Why are we going after just the Bartram Emeralds when most of Lady Jennifer's jewelry will be right there?" was the follow-up shortly after, and on another occasion it was, "How did you come up with the convoluted idea to do this in the first place?" And that was on top of the smaller, easier questions like "wouldn't it be easier to change this step here, or condense these five steps down into two?" that lurked around every corner.

Those, at least, Rodrigo could deal with, usually with a, "Hm, yes, let's do that instead". But there were no good answers for the big "why" questions, other than, "That's just the way we've always done it, because for reasons I can't explain, I've never felt like I had a choice to do otherwise".

Except that, somehow, he *did* feel like he had the choice now. Perhaps, if he got unreasonably lucky and that freedom ended up lasting, he could finally change all those things that Ellis questioned. He could find something different to do that wasn't a constant cycle of seduction and narrow escapes and that didn't make the rest of the crew put themselves in danger trying to make up the slack.

For now, he could finish the Lady Jennifer heist, and set his sights on something just slightly less drastic.

Like, just perhaps, admitting that he was falling for Amora Ellis more and more every day, and that he should consider doing something about that.

Chapter 13

If she were honest with herself, Latisha should have probably seen it coming.

She had been pleasantly surprised by the good bits of her worldbuilding—the denizens of the Bairn and Sparrowhawk, Rodrigo's latent decency—turning up from the depths of her long-abandoned first drafts.

Thus, it followed that some less savory elements would be waiting in the wings as well. But for the time being, she was so caught up in planning a heist *sensibly* for a change, in spending time with Rodrigo that—wonder of wonders—was actually enjoyable, that it didn't occur to her to worry about trouble not directly related to either of those things.

But now that she was paying attention to her surroundings and looking for things she'd missed instead of just trying to get by, she started to pick up on some less pleasant surprises.

It started the day that Grammy sent her with Asad on another errand. They were evidently in need of a replacement cross-head for the engine, and the most affordable source for it was in a part of town where Asad was reluctant to venture alone. Grammy almost immediately suggested that Latisha accompany him, citing the opportunity for her to explore more of the city. But the area they were walking through wasn't much to look at—even plainer and sketchier than where they'd gone on their earlier outing—so she found herself watching Asad instead.

She'd had other things on her mind when they ventured out before, and she hadn't known him as well then, either. Now, the tension in Asad's shoulders and stride was obvious, as was the way demeanor changed from the warm openness he displayed on the *Rake* to the wary quiet that had characterized him when she first arrived.

She could see the reasons for it more clearly, too. People who passed them on the street and heard Asad's quiet ticking would swerve widely around them, staring after them with distrust or outright hatred. A handful of rough-looking young men seemed to be following them a few yards behind, with a look in their eyes Latisha didn't trust.

"Are they going to try and attack us—you?" she asked quietly, with a subtle head tilt towards the group in question. "We can head back home if it's too dangerous."

Asad shook his head. "Not if they're smart. It takes someone pretty stupid to try and smash up a Verne for scrap. If I were alone, someone might try to start a fight, and that could get ugly if I hit back. But you're here, and human," he added bitterly, "so it should be fine."

Latisha's head was spinning with remembered, abandoned worldbuilding. In her published books, Asad's nature as an automaton had been barely mentioned. Before she'd sold out, though, she'd had pages upon pages of notes about automata in general and the typical disenfranchisement they faced.

She'd never used that lore, but she'd never directly contradicted it either—when would she have had the opportunity? As Evie would have told her, explorations of AI rights or discrimination didn't fit in the kind of romance novels she was meant to be selling.

She should have remembered before. She was seeing it clearly enough now, as they finally reached their destination and the shop's proprietor took one look and wouldn't let Asad enter, muttering nonsense about how he would "throw off the calibrations". The worst part was that Asad clearly expected this from previous visits, and didn't even try to protest.

Latisha explained what they needed and made it through the bargaining as best as she could, but suspected that Asad would have gotten them a lower price.

Outside, the young men who'd been following them were starting to circle closer, not engaging yet, but just about to. Latisha casually drew the knife she'd been provided with and held it ready in her hand as she and Asad started back. The group reluctantly dispersed, and there were no further outright incidents for the rest of the trip, but she could still feel the moment Asad relaxed once they set foot back on the *Rake*.

It wasn't just today, though—it was his whole life. She'd set up those circumstances, and the knowledge burned uncomfortably inside her as she tried to go about the rest of her day.

A few days later, while she was still trying to sort out her thoughts, she was pulled away from helping Grammy clean the galley by a commotion up on the deck. She scrambled up to investigate, with Rodrigo a few steps ahead of her, and was greeted by the sight of Ruby huddled on the deck close to tears while Linn held her and Asad hovered protectively over them. Both adults looked murderous.

Rodrigo voiced what everyone else was thinking. "What's going on? What happened?"

Linn practically snarled at him.

"She was out trying to lift some extra coin and almost got snatched by a Sourcer—probably from one of the mills outside town. He chased her clear from Corey Street to here. If we hadn't been watching for her and waiting with the rope ladder, he would have gotten her."

Latisha wanted to be sick. She'd thought it was a clever bit of wordplay when she came up with the idea of "human resources men", or Sourcers. They were people who kidnapped homeless children and other destitute individuals to work in the worst of the factories and mills.

She doubted anyone currently surrounding her would find the wordplay even mildly amusing.

When Rodrigo spoke, his voice was shaking. "That's it. Ruby, I'm sorry, but I mean it this time. You can't go out pickpocketing anymore. We'll find a way to make ends meet, but you can't be putting yourself in danger like this."

Ruby—sweet, irrepressible Ruby who wanted to go where no one had gone before—looked up angrily, her face streaked with tears. "The stealing wasn't what put me in danger. I was coming back, just walking down the wrong street. And if you want me to stop so badly, why don't you find a way to actually make some money besides your *stupid* heists!"

Rodrigo couldn't have looked more betrayed and hurt if she'd punched him in the gut, and he seemed to crumple further when Ruby glanced down and muttered, "Sorry," only for Asad to counter with, "No, don't apologize; you're right, and maybe this will finally make him see sense."

Since nobody was paying attention to Latisha at all, she elected to scurry back below before she would have to hear any more of what promised to be a spectacularly nasty fight. But she couldn't escape from the ugly silence at dinner that night, or from Ruby's muffled weeping in the cabin next door after she woke up from a nightmare.

Nor could she escape from the rapidly compounding guilt that seemed to be gathering new fuel at every turn—the incidents she'd witnessed, the darker facets of this society that she'd enacted and then never made arrangements to fix, and the trauma that all of them probably had that she'd never given them the opportunity to process.

If she'd been caught between a desire to stay and a desire to go home where she had the power to fix things, that would have been relatively easy.

But she wasn't sure she would even be able to put things right if she did manage to get home.

The final straw came a few days later, when Rodrigo insisted on borrowing her for a "quick errand".

It soon became clear—once they set foot on the skydocks he'd convinced Asad to tie up at—that the errand was a thin excuse to get off the ship for a couple of hours. While it hadn't taken long for everyone to start speaking to each other again after the incident with Ruby, the tension hadn't completely dissipated. Everyone seemed determined to hyperfocus on the upcoming ball and following heist, which meant that there wasn't a lot of space to hold onto grudges with so much to get done, but it was clear that Rodrigo wanted an escape from it.

Why he'd wanted her to come along, Latisha wasn't sure. She didn't think he'd ever hesitated to come and go alone when he wanted to in the past.

"Is there even an actual errand we need to do?" she asked. "Or are we just killing time?"

"A little of both," he said, aiming for carelessness and not quite reaching it. "I thought I ought to look into a potential next job for us, and out of my two best sources of common sense, you're more mobile at the moment, so I thought you ought to come along."

It sounded like something he'd rehearsed. Latisha thought about calling him on it and decided against it. Instead, she inquired, "How are we supposed to scope out a mark from up here?" If they were heading to ground level with her not in a ball gown, they would've taken the rope ladder instead of paying docking fees.

"As a matter of fact, we aren't scoping out a mark." He sounded more than a little triumphant about that fact. "I've been wanting to quit the heists and do something different for a while now, and if we find something now, we can go straight from one job to another without wasting time in between."

He didn't say anything about Linn's injury and Ruby's near-kidnapping being the impetus for his taking action right then, but Latisha had her suspicions anyway. Perhaps she should have pitied him for the guilt he was clearly carrying around over the financial predicament of his crew, but instead she felt mild envy.

At least *he* could do something to amend the situation and feel like he'd made up for it.

"So how exactly are we supposed to find a job? I assume people don't put up posters somewhere with 'Help wanted: skyship and crew of six to take care of some shady illegal business' printed on them."

That made him laugh. "Not as such. But if you go to the right places looking like the right sort of person, it's not too difficult to get hired."

The right place, in this instance, was evidently a pub much shadier-looking than the Bairn and Sparrowhawk, with a sign too dilapidated for Latisha to read. The smoky, grungy interior was filled with people hunched over the bar or stained tables, who were holding conversations in low mutters. Rodrigo's good cheer as he entered and steered her towards a corner table seemed wildly out of place.

Nobody approached them to make them order anything, which was just as well, because Latisha wasn't willing to consume anything from a place that stank like this without modern medical services readily available.

She directed a questioning look at Rodrigo, who shrugged, seeming to understand what she meant. "I don't have any coin, the ale here is terrible, and half the people who come here never order anything anyway. The criminal syndicates make sure this place stays open as long as it's convenient to them."

"*Mon Rodrigue,*" a low, honeyed feminine voice cut in, and Latisha swiveled around and blinked in shock at the woman sauntering up to their table.

She was the walking embodiment of every "sexy steampunk" trope that Latisha's family had ever despairingly pictured, kept from public indecency by her tall, stiletto-heeled boots and the mane of blonde hair that spilled over her shoulders and overabundant cleavage; it wasn't as if the scraps of silk and lace passing for a blouse and skirt were covering much. Her silver-blue eyes gleamed in the dim light as she dropped into a chair across from them, assorted pistols and blades clinking at every movement.

Rodrigo clearly recognized her. "Capitan Bonheur," he greeted stiffly.

Unfortunately, Latisha recognized her, too. Floriane Bonheur, captain of the *Sirène*, had been her one foray into trying something different with the Rakish Heart novels. In *The Taming of the Rake*, Floriane had contacted Rodrigo, having heard of his reputation, and offered him a partnership. She had a fence lined up for a particular item of jewelry, and all the information needed to get it out of its safe, but she needed Rodrigo to actually get in. The owner had some of the tightest security around, but she also had a weakness for dashing dark-eyed men sweeping her off her feet.

The crew had been hard up, so Rodrigo had taken the job. He'd gone through the motions of sweeping the mark off her feet, while in actuality falling hard into a torrid romance with Floriane herself. They'd fought constantly with as much passion as they put into everything else, and at the end, she stabbed him and left him for dead while taking off with the item he'd stolen for her.

At the time, Latisha had enjoyed writing it. She'd wanted, just once, to put Rodrigo through some of the misery he put her through with every book--even though she hadn't known he was real then.

Now, when she could see the knife that had almost killed him sticking out of Floriane's belt only a few feet away and could feel Rodrigo rigid beside her, desperate to not be near this woman, she was burningly angry at this interloper, and at herself.

"Oh, I should think we know each other better than that," Floriane purred, leaning forward slightly and rendering her blouse even less effective. "Even if it has been such a long time since we saw one another."

"I would have thought you'd have guessed that that was on purpose," Rodrigo snapped. "If I recall, you're clever enough with people's motives to work out that much."

"Now, don't be like that. I did come to offer you a job, after all, since I assumed by your presence here that you're looking for one."

Rodrigo fixed her with an icy glare. "There is no level of desperation I could sink to that would make me have any association with you. There is nothing I could ever want so badly that I would accept it from you, and no place I could want to be so badly that I would stay if you were there. Is that clear enough for you? I could go on."

In the weeks she'd lived in proximity to him, Latisha had come to see and appreciate several sides of Rodrigo that she'd never guessed at before, but this was the first time she'd seen him truly angry, and she could only be glad it wasn't directed at her.

She wasn't sure where Floriane found the nerve to not only stay put, but to flirtatiously reach across toward one of Rodrigo's hands, laughing softly. "I've missed seeing you angry, Rodrigue."

"He said for you to get lost," Latisha snapped.

Floriane's eyes flicked over to her in surprise.

"Who's this, then? Your little doxy? I would have thought you'd have better taste," she commented with noticeably more bite in her words.

Rodrigo stood up abruptly. "We're done here," he pronounced, reaching for Latisha's hand and pulling her to her feet as well. "If you know what's good for you, Bonheur, you won't come near me or my crew again."

With that, he marched out the door, hauling Latisha behind him until they were a few buildings away. Eventually, he ducked into a gap between a barber's and a pawnshop and slumped against one of the warped board walls, letting out a long, shaky breath.

Latisha joined him, cautiously. "Is everything all right?" she asked, which felt like a stupid question, but it was the only thing she could think of to say.

"We just can't go back there, is all," Rodrigo muttered. "Not now that she's seen us there. Probably best to steer clear of any places I might otherwise go looking for work, too. Blast it."

Belatedly, Latisha realized she wasn't meant to have any idea who Floriane was. "What's so bad about that woman knowing where to find you? It seemed like you had some kind of . . . history, but . . ."

"It's a long story." Rodrigo was staring into space in front of him rather than looking at her. "We worked together once. We were . . . close, or at least I thought so. But she turned on me and almost killed me, and now she's shown up acting like we'd just had a spat. I'd hoped neither I nor the crew would ever have to see her again, but clearly my luck isn't that good."

Every word was piling more and more guilt onto Latisha's shoulders, particularly since she suspected that Floriane was only part of the problem, and the larger issue was Rodrigo's attempted job hunt being nipped in the bud. She wanted to listen and help, but she wasn't sure if she could stand to hear anymore.

She took his hand and squeezed it. "Come on. We'd better get back to the *Rake* before she gets the idea to follow us."

They made it back without further trouble and Rodrigo got Asad to get them underway with a minimum of explanations. Latisha just leaned on the railing, looking out at the sky and wrestling with her thoughts.

What had happened today had been worse than the other incidents, somehow. She hadn't just made Floriane do those things that had hurt Rodrigo; she'd done them herself—manipulated him and caused him harm, and then shown up in his life as if she had any right to do so.

Perhaps it wasn't quite the same, since she hadn't known better, but she suddenly wasn't so sure Rodrigo would see it that way.

And without her realizing it, somewhere between his giving her a job and a home and the dancing and the sparring and the trust he'd placed in her . . . Rodrigo turning that betrayed, righteous anger on her had become something she would do anything to avoid.

There was, just possibly, a very slight chance that she should admit to herself that she'd developed feelings for him.

Of course, that conclusion would come at the end of a week that proved just how little he would want anything to do with her if he knew the truth about who she was.

Chapter 14

It was just about typical of Rodrigo's luck that just when he thought he might be connecting with Ellis--might be getting somewhere with her, preferably the kind of somewhere that he could finally confess his growing feelings for her—she started to draw back into herself again.

She still did all the things she'd been doing before, such as helping Grammy, taking self-defense lessons from him, chatting with Ruby, and working with the others to plan the heist. On paper, nothing really changed.

But she was more subdued these days, no longer cheerfully poking holes in his favorite tactics or flashing distracting smiles at him when they sparred. It was almost like when she first arrived on the *Rake*, before she trusted him, but Rodrigo couldn't think of anything he might have done to lose her trust.

It came to him late one night when he was trying to sleep, as these things sometimes did. Ellis' behavior had begun to change shortly after their run-in with Floriane. He hadn't thought there was any connection at the time, but now he found he couldn't discount the possibility. He'd had experiences before where a mark's suspicious parent or older brother would drag an old flame back into the picture, in an attempt to get his target to cast Rodrigo over.

It hadn't ever worked, but perhaps it had worked on Ellis. Perhaps Floriane had intimidated her and made her want to back away from whatever they'd been building towards. He wouldn't have thought Ellis was susceptible to such tactics, but you could never tell with people. Linn, the most level-headed person he knew, had been positively flighty where Asad was concerned until they sorted things out and began courting.

Perhaps something like that was the solution here, too. He just needed to find an opportunity to talk things out with her, and then they could go back to being comfortable with one another and get this heist over with. Then maybe, just maybe, they could figure out a new line of work after that.

It was a wonderful plan, as two-in-the-morning plans went. Unfortunately, in the daylight hours, things became rather more complicated.

The trouble was, he'd neglected to consider that his habitual approach to romantic endeavors was circuitous and laden with misdirection. He caught her in the hall after breakfast that morning, fully intending to have a straightforward discussion along the lines of "I fancy you terribly. Do you return the sentiment, or have I completely misread things?"

Instead, what he found himself saying was, "I've been meaning to ask, do you want to write to your family and let them know where you are and how you're doing? Not about the heist, obviously, but it's perfectly possible to keep up correspondence with landsiders without anyone getting arrested, if you send from the right fuel docks. Asad writes to his uncles and would probably lend you things if you ask."

Which wasn't the worst way he could have started out. He could see himself working around to the topic he actually meant to talk about in a dozen conversational moves or so.

"Um. Thanks. But I don't think I will."

Unless she did that.

Ellis tugged on one of her curls that had come loose. "It's just . . . I sort of said before, I haven't really been in touch with them in a while. Or they haven't been in touch with me. Didn't bother after they assumed the worst about what I was doing to get by. They said it was immoral, even though I never actually—but anyway, suffice to say, I won' t be needing to borrow Asad's stuff."

Rodrigo had lived in the criminal and semi-legal world long enough to be aware of any number of things a person could have been doing to survive that would fit that scattered description. He was sure that Ellis wanted him poking into precisely none of it, so he settled for saying, "I'm sorry. Forget I said anything."

"It's all right, you meant well." She'd had her eyes on the floor, and now glanced up at him. "I miss them, but . . . I haven't as much since I came here. Maybe because I've been keeping so busy, I don't know. Is that wrong?"

"Of course not." He crossed to lean against the wall beside her. "I would hope that living on a skyship and keeping busy preparing for a heist day in and day out would be enough to distract anyone from thinking about unpleasant things. And—" He took a deep breath, sensing an opportunity, but not wanting to muff this business of comforting reassurance for the sake of a cheap maneuver. "I would hope that you'd prefer it here, with people who appreciate you, over somewhere where the people around you are only trying to find fault with you."

She seemed about to reply, but before she could, he heard Asad call, "Captain, you got a minute? Need to see you about something."

Whenever Asad 'needed to see him about something', it was usually an urgent engineering problem that couldn't be put off.

He muttered something along the lines of, "Sorry, got to go," to Ellis, then hurried off towards the engine room. The 'something' he was needed for turned out to merely be taking Asad's side on a rare argument over the parts budget with Linn, who he swore he heard saying something about a "five-point penalty for interference" when he walked in.

This might have made him more suspicious under other circumstances, but as it was, his mind was occupied with trying to figure out some new way to approach Ellis.

He'd never thought of the *Rake* as small or crowded, but when it took him until a couple of evenings thereafter to catch her alone again, he was beginning to have second thoughts.

This seemed perfect, though: she was out on the deck, leaning on the railing and looking out at the sunset-stained clouds. Everything was calm, and everyone else was busy with their various tasks.

He came up slowly and took up a place at the railing beside her, and she didn't object.

"It's beautiful," she commented, gesturing out at the sky.

That was too good to pass up. "Very beautiful," he agreed, straight-faced and looking directly at her.

Considering that she immediately started blushing and couldn't seem to meet his gaze, she knew exactly what he was doing.

Momentarily riding high on the small victory of having successfully flirted with someone he didn't mean to rob—and with Ellis, no less—he went to pursue his advantage but pulled up short when he realized that she looked like she was trying not to cry.

"Is everything all right?" he inquired.

"I don't know. Some things are, and some things aren't, and the things that are . . . feel like they shouldn't be." She shook herself slightly. "Don't mind me, I'm not making sense. I just ramble sometimes when I'm tired."

Well, it was true that he wasn't sure what she was talking about, but he did want to know. "Why shouldn't things be all right?"

She was still staring into space rather than looking at him. "I don't know. Maybe it's that all of this doesn't quite feel real sometimes. I'll wake up some mornings and think I'm back where I used to be, before the *Rake*, and it takes me a second to remember."

"Was it that bad where you were before?"

"Not bad, necessarily, just . . . " She shifted to face him. "Have you ever . . . ever started something that didn't seem like a big deal

105

at the time, that you figured you would just do and be done with it, but then it doesn't stop when you expected it to, and it just . . . snowballs? And then it takes over your whole life. And after a point, you look back and realize it's been a part of your life for so long that you don't think to change it, even if it makes you miserable? It was like that."

Rodrigo was nodding before he even thought about it, because that was almost the perfect description of how the heists had begun and gone on. "I know just what you mean."

According to everything he knew, that was supposed to be a Right Thing to say, so he was caught off guard when Ellis turned away, something in her expression shuttering. She pulled away like she'd been doing for days.

He reached out for her, trying to get her to turn back to him and searching for something he could say to right the situation. "Look. Ellis. I don't know the details of what your life was like before you came here. I don't need to ever know if you don't want to tell me. But that doesn't have to define you now. You can make anything you like of yourself up here. You can do whatever you want. That's what makes a skydweller—just someone who's looking for a chance at a new life."

But she only jerked away from his touch, moving away from him and towards the deck hatch. "You don't understand," she spat. "Just leave me alone and mind your own business, you've got enough of it."

Then she was gone, leaving Rodrigo alone by the rail with the disquieting sensation of having lost a fight without knowing that it was happening or what it was about.

There was another ball on the schedule three days after the not-fight, and despite Rodrigo's best efforts, he was unable to mend relations with Ellis even a little. She avoided him as much as possible and was never alone with him until they actually had to leave and catch a clock-carriage. By then it was too late to do anything but focus on the job and hope she wouldn't disappear before he could get things sorted.

The one upside was that whatever she was angry at him for did wonders for her ability to play the shrewish fiancée. She stage-whispered some of the most biting invective he'd ever heard throughout the first three dances—a pity, since she was now moving with him far more naturally than she had on their first escapade—to the point where it was rather difficult to find anyone else to hand her off to at the proper time.

He was only able to disengage and move on Lady Jennifer thanks to the timely interception of a sorry-looking young fop with a hearing problem who had no idea what she was saying.

A pity, Rodrigo reflected as he spun Lady Jennifer through a dazzling turn, taking advantage of her momentary inattention to seek out Ellis as he'd been doing throughout the evening. Under better circumstances and when not playing a role, she was a delight to talk to. The fop didn't know what he was missing.

It was the watching her that made him think of it, some time later. Ellis went from the fop to another partner and another, moving through the room with far more confidence than on her first outing. All she needed was time and practice, and she'd be a good enough con woman to make her own way if she ever decided she wanted to. And now that she was so distant, it occurred to him, what was to stop her from wanting to? She was close with the crew, yes, but presumably she'd been close with her family once upon a time, and she'd found a way to live without them when she needed to. There was nothing to stop her leaving the *Rake* someday, sooner rather than later if he didn't fix whatever had gone wrong.

So, he needed to fix it as soon as he could.

Tonight, if possible.

Chapter 15

Latisha knew that Rodrigo knew something was up with her. He'd kept trying to talk to her alone, but any time they talked anymore, everything got more complicated and twisted around in her head.

He was just so very real, against all sense or logic, but she'd *made* him with her often-thoughtless words. And despite this, she thought she might love him, or at least be on the way to it—she'd loved him a long time ago, after all, as a creator loves the thing they create, and now that she'd met him, she was starting to love him for the person he'd always been despite her.

But that brought it right back to the part where she'd made a mess of his life, and that brought on the guilt, and then he tried to *comfort her.*

At that point she was too angry with herself to be near him and his well-meaning obliviousness any longer.

She wasn't an idiot; she knew he'd been flirting with her for a while now, but she hoped that a few days' unexplained avoidance would cause him to back off gracefully. Perhaps she should have known that a man with the tenacity to have spent ten years running down a dream of flight wouldn't give up so easily.

But now he was getting distracted by her when they were on the job instead of focusing on Lady Jennifer, and that was something she couldn't just ignore. The heist was in a couple of weeks, and she wasn't in control. They needed to be on point—him especially.

So once the ball had finished and they'd hailed a clock-carriage back to the docks, she took the seat across from him, glared, and asked, "What was wrong with you tonight? You kept watching me, and if I noticed clear across the room, I know Lady Jennifer did."

Irritatingly, he didn't even bother to deny it. "If you expect me to apologize for being concerned for your well-being, you'll be sorely disappointed," he contended, arms folded.

"My well-being is not the point!" Latisha snapped. "The point is that we were there to do a job —"

"The job is replaceable," he interrupted. "You are not. Looking after you—or anyone else on my crew—always takes priority."

"I don't need you to look after me. I was handling things just fine."

"Handling the people in there just fine, yes. But if going out of your way to avoid me for three days for no apparent reason is what you call 'fine', we must be working with different definitions of the word."

There was no good answer she could give him for that, none that didn't involve spilling everything, at least. She was exhausted, and she had, alarmingly, *missed* him during the past few days of avoidance.

And now he was making this fight about her rather than about him, and so without really thinking it through, she muttered, "You keep talking about your crew's well-being, but what if there's a conflict? One person's welfare versus everyone else's?"

Because that was what all the twisted-around back-and-forth in her head came down to—she was, in her less guilty moments, happier here than she'd ever thought she could be. She slept better on her lumpy cot than she had before in her life, and she hardly noticed the ever-present smell of smoke anymore. She was more comfortable with her five tightly-packed shipmates than she'd ever been with another group of people.

And yet as long as she was in this world, the flaws she'd woven into it had no chance of being fixed.

Rodrigo, however, was clearly on a different wavelength. "Floriane was a mistake," he sighed, "one I've learned from and won't let happen again."

"What? What does that have to do with Floriane?" Her bewilderment was genuine—she had no clue how he'd made that leap.

"What else would you mean by —" The penny seemed to drop, at least partially. "Ellis, if you're talking about yourself—you haven't done anyone on the crew any harm. I don't think you could, barring accidents."

She fought the insane urge to laugh. "You don't understand— and please don't try to make me explain; I can't."

Instead of backing off, he naturally took this as an invitation to forge ahead and unintentionally make her feel worse. "Is this why . . .? If you're in some kind of trouble, you can tell me. We won't throw you out. We can protect you."

She should have known he would assume she was in some kind of mysterious danger. It would make a tidy explanation for her behavior lately, and if she'd had the energy, she might have leaned into it, but she was too worn out to conjure more unwieldy backstory from thin air.

"Just . . . just leave it alone, okay? It's not your business, and all . . . this—" She gestured at him. "—this being sweet and helpful about my problems for no reason is only making things more difficult."

He blinked in confusion. "Making sure my partner in crime isn't about to have a breakdown or get caught by some unspecified troublesome past isn't sweet. It's just good sense," he asserted. "I admit I might have more personal motivations involved as well, but you'll forgive me for wanting to make sure the woman I love isn't in mortal peril —" He cut himself off abruptly.

For a moment, everything seemed frozen except for her racing pulse, and Latisha couldn't seem to find her voice. He'd just . . . said it, like it was a matter of fact and not something that was shaking her to her core. "What—you can't —"

Watching Rodrigo decide to go for broke was a process. First, he balked, then quietly berated himself while looking away from her gaping face. But then he seemed to steel himself as he came to some sort of internal decision.

He reached out and took her hands in his, smiling a little sheepishly. "Ellis, I haven't been able to keep my eyes or my mind off you since you started working with me on this job. You're hardworking, clever, and a born infiltrator, and you've put together the best plan we've had for a heist in years. Is it so strange that I would fall in love with you?"

In no version of reality could she have ever expected to hear those words from him, and yet Latisha couldn't deny their truthfulness. She'd seen it, for days and weeks now, in words and looks and little actions that she'd tried to brush off as meaningless. The truth was clear in his dark eyes, which were now gazing at her with an affection she couldn't misconstrue.

He meant every word, and it was terrifying.

The carriage was too quiet. She registered that they'd come to a stop, meaning that they were back at the skydocks. Without thinking, she tore her hands out of Rodrigo's grasp, fumbled behind her at the door until it swung open, and flung herself out, running for the stairs that would take her back to the *Rake*. With any luck, Rodrigo would get held up paying the driver long enough for her to get up and into her cabin, where she could hide until morning. By then, hopefully all this would have gone away.

The captain was swearing somewhere behind her, but she kept running, trying not to think and failing miserably. She wanted to tell him she'd been falling for him, too. She wanted to let him pull her into a kiss and find out if kissing him was all it was cracked up to be in the overly florid, corset-melting passages she'd written too many of.

But that was just the problem.

She'd written him. She'd written him being with other women, occasions that she knew far too much about. What would it say about her that she had fallen in love with a man she'd invented? What would it say about her that she wanted a relationship with a man whose flaws and criminal history and ridiculously long string of exes were her fault?

Not to mention that he had no idea who she really was, and she could never, ever tell him the truth. And there was a non-zero chance that she could at any moment be pulled back to her native world with as little explanation as she'd arrived—though that was looking less and less likely with each day that passed.

She made it to the deck of the *Rake* but was forced to pause, bent over, to catch her breath. The lacing of this particular corset allowed for some fairly athletic dancing, but not for deranged sprints.

Unfortunately, this allowed Rodrigo the few seconds he needed to also reach the deck and approach her. She was miffed to notice that he was much less winded than she was.

"I have to say," he uttered dryly, "I was prepared for a wide range of reactions when I finally told you I loved you, but actually running away was not something I anticipated."

Perhaps it was unfair, but lacking any other ideas, she elected to turn the argument back on him. "Of course. I forgot. Your experience. Just how many women—not counting me—have you claimed to love?" She knew the answer, but that wasn't the point.

Rodrigo, to his credit, looked slightly abashed. "Ellis, the heists . . ."

"Are you going to tell me they don't count?" She had no right to be asking him these things, but she couldn't stop. If she stopped, she would have to let his assertion of—of *loving* her stand, and she could accept that even less.

"No. It's worse than that." He started pacing, one hand running through his hair. "You've asked me before why I do the heists and

112

why I set them up the way I do. I told you at the time that I didn't know, but I didn't explain just how true that is. When I choose a mark and start setting them up and making plans, it's like I'm not fully in control of myself. Some of the time, it'll feel like I'm making my own decisions, but only about little things. Other times, I'll almost be watching myself do and say things that I would never want to. I'll dance with some woman and kiss her and tell her she's beautiful and rob her and break her heart, and I will have absolutely no clue why."

With every word, the twisted regret and self-hatred she'd been flirting with for the last few days continued to grow. This—this, too, was her fault.

He came to a halt, and looked at her, eyes wild. "I know the crew thinks I'm an idiot for keeping on doing this. I've tried to stop or do other things. But it never lasts long, and then the compulsion comes back, and everything's upended again. I know it sounds crazy, but I swear it's the truth. Have I told several other women before that I loved them? Yes. Did I want to in any way, shape, or form? No."

Silence hung between them, broken only by the faint creaking of the ship. Latisha shoved her recriminations deep inside and forced herself to remain calm as she asked. "What about this heist?"

"It started out like all the others." Rodrigo shrugged helplessly. "Then, the day you arrived . . . I don't know what happened, but as I walked away from talking to Lady Jennifer, I could feel I was in control of myself again. Ever since then, every choice I've made has been my own. I don't know what changed. I can't even promise that whatever it was won't come back." He stepped towards her, closing the distance between them, and rested his hands carefully on her upper arms.

Her heart cracked at the fact that his grip was loose enough that she could still break away if she wanted to. How could she have ever thought that this caring, respectful, and spirited man was such a reprobate?

Rodrigo's palms were warm against her bare skin. "Amora Ellis, I swear that everything I have felt—and continue to feel—for you is true and honest. Nothing has compelled me to fall in love with you."

The way he looked at her could break the heart of a lesser woman. Who knew—maybe it could happen to her, too, with the way her life had been going lately.

She was Latisha Robbins, writer of tacky romance novels. Yet here she was standing on a flying ship in a steampunk city in a dress fit for a minor noble . . . and she had fallen in love with a reluctant rake from another world who loved her back.

Giving in didn't necessarily make sense, but then again, her life had stopped making sense a long time ago.

She was tired, more than anything, of holding back so much. Holding back in her writing, holding back her secrets, and holding back the feelings she couldn't deny any longer.

Not letting herself stop to think about it, Latisha took one step forward and threaded her arms around Rodrigo's neck, kissing him—

—*And within a heartbeat, he was kissing her back, strong arms wrapping around her as his mouth plundered hers -*

No.

With effort, she forced her auto-narrator to hush. She wasn't Floriane, or Adhara, or Saoirse, or Nayeli or any of the exotically beautiful characters he'd done this with before. She was just herself, and that was apparently good enough, because she was the one he'd chosen. He was kissing her with a jubilation she hadn't thought possible.

This moment was just theirs, and she wasn't going to sully it with comparisons to his past, transient encounters.

When he gently pulled away a few seconds later, it felt far too soon. Latisha tried to pull him back in, slightly dizzy from the hormone-laden blood pounding through her head. If she was going to toss aside all her rules and do this sappy romance-heroine thing, she was going to do it properly, and she'd only just been getting started.

He startled, looking over her shoulder. She whirled to see what had spooked him, only to see that Linn had joined them and was standing by the hatch, arms crossed and looking, of all things, smug.

"I can explain—" Latisha started to say, abruptly aware that the man she'd just been caught making out with had been Linn's best friend from childhood, only to cut herself off when Rodrigo, at the same time, commented a trifle breathlessly, "Some blasted timing, Linn."

The first mate just laughed. "I thought I heard a commotion and came up to check, but clearly you had things well in hand." Her focus shifted to Rodrigo. "Since I'm up anyway, any chance you could catch me up on what I missed from tonight's escapade?"

It was an invitation that could have technically been for both of them, but Latisha knew better—Linn wanted to talk with her friend and captain alone, presumably about the new development she'd just walked in on.

Latisha wasn't going to stand in the way of that. "Rodrigo should be able to fill you in," she spoke up. "I'll just . . . head to bed. It's been a long day."

Both nodded, but Rodrigo pulled her close for a moment before letting her go, softly saying "She's not angry with either of us. Tomorrow, we'll talk and get this sorted out, all right?"

Latisha nodded, then made for the hatch.

Despite the embarrassment and the trepidation, she couldn't help but feel somewhat giddy, delighted even.

She'd kissed Rodrigo, and the world hadn't ended, and while there were definitely going to be complications and fallout, she wanted to believe that maybe this wouldn't turn into a horrible disaster.

As she headed for her cabin, light unexpectedly flared up behind her, causing her to turn.

Grammy emerged into the corridor, carrying an oil lamp and frowning at her.

"So," she said, clearly, but quietly enough to not be heard up on deck, "you finally gave in to him."

Latisha blinked. "How did you—never mind, I don't care. Can we talk about it tomorrow?"

"No. If it could, do you think I'd be up at nearly one in the morning?" Grammy retorted. "I know who you are, and I know what brought you here. You're a scrivener, and you haven't exactly been honest with that lovestruck idiot who just kissed you."

Latisha's desire to escape the conversation vanished. If Grammy's words meant what she thought they did, this might be the closest she'd get to finding answers. With more information, she might be able to figure out how and why she'd fallen into this world in the first place and what might cause her to leave or stay.

Grammy was right—this couldn't wait until morning.

Her train of thought must have showed on her face because Grammy nodded sharply and pulled her along, expression grim. "Galley, now. Let's not wake up the others."

Chapter 16

"So," Linn said, after Ellis had made her exit and the silence had stretched out to a rather uncomfortable length, "you finally managed to tell her, I see."

She said it with a wry twist of humor, rather than any kind of condemnation, so Rodrigo didn't fight the slightly foolish grin creeping onto his face. "And it was worth any amount of 'I told you so's, so you needn't bother."

"I won't—although given how you acted when Asad and I were courting, I maintain I'd be well within my rights to give you all manner of grief. Fortunately for you, I happen to be the non-retaliatory kind."

Rodrigo could have countered with half a dozen examples to the contrary, but those were all involving people outside of the crew who'd done actual harm, and he knew what she meant.

He could also tell that she hadn't quite said everything she wanted to. "Did you really want to hear what Ellis and I got up to at the ball tonight, or did you have something else you wanted to discuss?"

"Well, I originally waited up to get a status update, but now, as it turns out, I do have something more pressing in mind." She sighed, glanced at the open hatch, kicked it shut as if to deter eavesdroppers, and moved closer to him. "Rodrigo, are you sure about her? As sure as it's possible to be about someone, anyway?"

"Of course, I am," he answered automatically, a bit startled.

Then, "Why shouldn't I be?"

"No reason at all. I'm not asking if you trust her, because if you didn't, she wouldn't be here in the first place. I'm asking if you're sure you want to try and make this work. If you're serious about it, or if it's just some passing thing."

The question caught him off guard for a moment—he hadn't been thinking about any kind of long-term future. He did his best not to think too far into the future in general, because such trains of thought tended to get depressing rather quickly.

Yet, even though he couldn't honestly say he had any idea of a specific future with Ellis, he had gotten the sense that whatever was between them had the potential to grow into something permanent, provided she ever acquiesced to such a thing.

He'd never had that sense before with any of the various marks he'd played at romance with, or even with Floriane—they'd certainly had something, but he had always known deep down that she wasn't the kind to stay.

He had known Linn would be a permanent fixture in his life from the moment they met, but aside from some adolescent confusion, that bond had become more akin to one of siblings. It'd been a hard realization at the time, but a good one, and he knew now that after the life she'd come from, she needed a steady and dependable man like Asad to hold her heart anyway.

He and Ellis could be good together like that, he knew, and it would be worth the effort.

"I am," he said, looking Linn in the eye. "I am sure about her. I don't know if she's in the same place, but —"

"She is," Linn interrupted. "I've seen her these past couple of weeks, and when she was avoiding you, and just now. She's crazy about you and trying not to be because she's afraid of being hurt or . . . something, anyway. Now I love you more than anyone alive besides my husband, so I'm telling you this once: if you break that woman's heart, you will live to regret it more than you've ever regretted anything."

Rodrigo raised an eyebrow. "I would've thought you'd be giving her the threats and so forth."

"I wasn't threatening you. I was warning you about natural consequences. I wouldn't even have to do anything." Linn gave him a hard stare. "Please tell me you understand that this means you have to give up doing the heists like you do. I know you've always insisted that you can't stop and that it's not your choice, but it had better be your choice pretty soon. I've seen how you are with marks, and I'm not sure any self-respecting woman would stay with someone who keeps doing that time and again."

He . . . honestly hadn't thought that through in much detail yet, but now that she'd said it, it was painfully obvious. "Do you know, I think I might actually be able to stop. I don't know what changed, but something did. I was starting to think about making a change, anyway—I just hadn't had the chance to do anything about it yet."

There was no need to mention Floriane showing up. That shouldn't happen again, and he would get other chances to look for alternative work. It would, he considered, be a pretty decent adventure in itself, finding something new to do.

"Maybe I could join you and Asad with your burglaries," he continued. "Or we could find something completely different to do —what was it we used to talk about when we were kids, before we got the *Rake*? I know it wasn't . . . this."

Linn grinned faintly in what might be relief. "I'm not sure I remember. Some of it was pretty fanciful, though, I think."

"It couldn't be worse nonsense than we've been living for the past several years." Rodrigo yawned abruptly, the energy from the ball and from Ellis kissing him abandoning him in a rush. "Is that all you needed to ask me about? Because I find I'm flat worn out, and it would seem there's a lot going on tomorrow."

"Like *some* of us getting up at a reasonable hour so we can leave before we have to pay another whole day's docking fees," Linn commented, smirking. "Good night, then. And good luck."

As he made his way down the corridor to his cabin, Rodrigo was just barely alert enough to notice light and the quiet murmur of Ellis and Grammy's voices coming from beneath the closed galley door. Strange that the latter should be up at this hour—she normally went to bed early, rose around dawn, and slept like a rock in between—but a deviance in someone's sleeping habits was hardly the strangest thing to happen to him.

He resolved to ask Ellis about it in the morning when he saw her and took himself off to his bunk for a well-earned sleep.

Chapter 17

Despite the urgency with which she'd called for this late-night meeting, Grammy didn't immediately elaborate on what she'd started to say.

She'd pulled Latisha into the galley and sat her down on one of the long benches at the table, then proceeded to make her way around the room and light several of the lamps from the candlestick in her hand.

Minutes later, she finally blew said candlestick out and sat herself on the opposite side of the table. Long seconds passed before either woman spoke—Grammy seemed unable to stop staring at Latisha in fascination.

Finally, Latisha cleared her throat. "Sorry, but what was it you needed to tell me so urgently? You've had weeks to look at me; if that's all you're going to do, I'd really rather just go clean up and sleep."

Grammy shook herself slightly. "Right, of course. It's just that I always thought a scrivener would look different, somehow, if I ever met one. But you just look like anybody I might pass on the street."

The euphoria of finally kissing Rodrigo notwithstanding, there was only so much drama she could take in one evening. "What's a scrivener, and what makes you think I'm one? Actually, how long have you thought that?"

"I knew as soon as I saw you," Grammy tossed out casually.

"When I came up on the deck and saw you all flopped over pretending to faint. It wasn't a very good performance, by the way, but considering you've stretched these people's suspension of disbelief to the breaking point, I'm not surprised you got away with it."

There was . . . a lot to process there. "What do you mean, *I* stretched their suspension of disbelief?" Latisha asked cautiously.

Grammy scoffed. "You know exactly what I mean. *You* wrote this world into existence, and you've known that you're in a world you made since the moment you got here. That's what a scrivener is."

"Wait a minute . . ." None of this was making any sense. "You're saying finding out that your fictional world is real is a *known phenomenon*? That this has happened to other people, to the point that there's a *name* for it?"

"That's exactly what I'm saying," Grammy confirmed, leaning forward to look Latisha in the eye. "Scriveners have the gift of making the worlds they write about real. Although 'known phenomenon' is a strong term—people in subcreated worlds like this have no clue, of course. Most scriveners have no idea either, and never find out. A few, like you, make an impromptu visit and learn the truth."

Latisha had a hundred questions on the tip of her tongue, but the one that made its way out was, "Does that have anything to do with why I couldn't manage to tell anyone my real name when I showed up here?"

"Oh, so that's a pen name. I thought 'Amora' was a little on the nose," Grammy snorted. "Amora Ellis is the name you gave yourself to write these stories, so that's the name you have here. That might change, though, if Rodrigo ever manages to get away from the heists and back to whatever you had in mind for him before."

"Before? How—how do you know about that?" Latisha demanded, trying to sound assertive and not like she'd just been exposed.

"I remember things," Grammy said impassively. "I've been around a long time. I was the grumpy neighbor who started a fight with Linn's trash heap of a stepfather to help her get away that night. I was going to be the old woman Rodrigo helped get home out of the rain, to show him he could still do good in the world. I was going to kiss his hands and bless him when he brought money from his first job 'round the slum. Even if those things haven't happened now, they had happened once, and Demodocus remembers."

"I'm sorry—what remembers?"

"Not what, who. A person, I suppose you could say, although I wouldn't. Demodocus is nothing so corporeal." Grammy tapped her temple with one bony finger. "It's in my head. It always has been, as long as I can remember. It can't do anything, but it knows everything worth knowing. It knows all the scriveners and all the worlds out there, and because I share my head with it, I can see, too, when I want to."

The old woman's eyes took on a faraway look. "I can't see into your world, so I didn't know who you were until you showed up. But I do appreciate the chance for a change of scenery every now and then. There's terrible worlds out there, overrun with monsters or collapsing under too many contradictions. But there's beautiful places, too—ancient green woods full of magic, or tall mountains, or cities with machines that don't smoke up the sky."

Latisha felt she should say something, to make up for her world not being any of the wonderful things Grammy had described, but instead found herself asking, "So does every book out there have a whole universe based on it?" Several dozen books flitted past in Latisha's mind—classics she'd endured or enjoyed in school, romances she'd skimmed to learn the tropes of her trade, the mystery novel she'd read on the bus several months back. "Oh, please tell me that's not a thing."

Her own characters might have had a hard time of it, but she didn't know if she could stand learning there was a world where Steinbeck's stuff had come to life.

"None of the ones here, or in any other scrivenworld," Grammy explained. "And even where you come from, not every writer gets the gift of scrivening. Quite a few aren't really imagining a new world in what they write—only what could happen in their own world. Others just don't quite connect to their worlds and their characters the way they'd need to bring them to life." Grammy shrugged, as if she wasn't completely upending Latisha's worldview. "My best guess is that you loved—truly loved—these idiots and their world at some point, back at the beginning, and by the time whatever went wrong happened, you'd already made them real."

"I'm sorry," Latisha managed. "Not for making it all real, I mean, but for messing things up."

Grammy brushed it off. "You could have made things a lot worse. But that's not what I brought you in here to talk about. What we need to talk about is Rodrigo."

Perhaps a little defensively, Latisha asked, "What about him?"

"He's in love with you," Grammy proclaimed bluntly.

"I know, he was just telling me. Why, are you going to try and tell me I have to go up to him tomorrow and tell him it was all a big mistake? Because I'm not going to do that. I've hurt him enough already."

"No." Grammy's gaze was steady and unrelenting. "I'm going to tell you that you have to leave."

Deep silence, except for the faint clicking of the ship's machinery somewhere far away. "Excuse me?"

"You're going to leave and go back to the world you came from, and you're going to do it tonight, before the captain falls any harder for you."

Surely, she'd heard wrong. Anger was quick on the heels of her disbelief. "Are you implying that I somehow made Rodrigo fall in love with me? Because I really didn't. I didn't even want this to happen until very, very recently. I don't have any scrivener superpowers here—I can't even manage to tell people my real name!"

"I know you didn't make him. That man would have lost his heart to you regardless, just because of who you are—an intelligent, brave, hardworking woman who makes him do better and doesn't care that he's pretty. Or at least won't admit to caring," Grammy added, throwing Latisha a sharp sideways look. "It doesn't mean you're weak that you're as susceptible to his looks as any other young woman. Even Linn had an eye on him for a bit, 'til Asad came along and turned out to be twice the man Captain was. But I digress. You can't stay here."

"First of all, I just told you I'm not going to hurt him any more. Second, I don't have a clue how to go back where I came from. If I did, I would've gone weeks ago." *Before somebody could give me a reason to stay*, she thought.

In those all-too-short moments between kissing Rodrigo and being intercepted by Grammy, she'd allowed herself to daydream about what her life might look like going forward, if she were allowed to stay and they made this work.

Maybe Rodrigo would stop the heisting and find a different line of work. Maybe they would still heist but find a different way to go about it. They would kiss and flirt openly and fight and make up. She would learn how to shoot, how to fly the ship, how to haggle with Monachus and his ilk. The *Rake* would fully become her home and the crew her family.

She could see herself living the rest of her life here, as Rodrigo's partner and lover—and maybe-someday-wife, if only to annoy Floriane.

Nowhere in all those daydreams was somebody supposed to say, "You have to leave."

She'd known it could happen, but she hadn't wanted to believe in it. Not anymore.

"Did you really think I would tell you you had to go home and not tell you how?" Grammy retorted. "Not every scrivener travels to their created worlds—it takes an emergency or a strong emotional connection. Demodocus brought you here without your trying because you were needed here. The crew was barely surviving with how you were telling the story, and you needed to see it in order to change or stop it. But unless I'm mistaken, you haven't been able to go back because there isn't anything there you care about strongly enough."

This, unfortunately, was something else Latisha couldn't argue with. She'd lied to Rodrigo about a lot, but she hadn't lied about losing touch with her family over how she made a living. After the third awkward Christmas dinner where her parents had talked around her job like she'd taken up exotic dancing—and one great-aunt actually called her several ugly names—she'd mostly let communication die out.

The person she saw most regularly was her agent, and Evie's cheerfully mercenary outlook and shameless, bubbly lust after Rodrigo tended to make Latisha's teeth itch.

"And now Demodocus can't send me back on another involuntary trip because I . . ." She paused, refusing to use what was probably the most accurate word. ". . . care about Rodrigo too much."

"Exactly."

"So, if my strong positive emotional connection to someone here can't be overcome by the omniscient entity that lives in your head, and no such connection exists with anyone where I came from, why should I leave?"

"Think about it." Grammy reached out and wrapped her hands around Latisha's, not letting her pull away. "Just how long do you think you can lie to him? He loves you, probably more deeply than he's ever been allowed to care for anybody before, and if you don't love him now, you will. Do you really want to try and see how long you can hide something this fundamental from him? You're not a woman who would let things get even this far without thinking about the long term. Do you honestly plan to let him court you, marry him, live a whole life with him, and lie to him the entire time?"

"So, I'll tell him," she said with more confidence than she felt. "I'll tell him everything tomorrow. We'll figure it out."

"And then he'll think you're joking. Or that you're insane. Or he'll believe you, and think he needs to treat you like some kind of goddess. Or he'll believe you and hate you for what you did to him. In any case, once he knows—if he takes you seriously at all— you won't be able to stay on the ship."

Once again, Latisha wanted to deny that the words were true, but couldn't quite convince herself otherwise.

"So, what's your magic solution?" she snapped. "According to you, I can't be with Rodrigo unless I tell him the truth, in which case I'd have to leave the Rake. But because I want to be with Rodrigo, your mystical mind link buddy can't send me back the way I came."

"That love for Rodrigo doesn't have to hold you here," Grammy countered. "And don't try to tell me it's not that—you obviously love him, but there's other ways to show that than hanging around here. If you go back where you came from, you could make this world better. I know you've been thinking about it. You could write stories that put Floriane Bonheur somewhere she can't bother anyone anymore and fix the way automata and street children are treated. Not to mention keeping the crew financially solvent for a change."

"I . . . " She *had* been thinking about it, but that train of thought always ended with sickening doubt that she could ever write Rodrigo again now that she knew him. "I'd never be able to get that published."

"What makes you think that'd make a difference? It's the writing that shapes the world, not the publishing of it."

"And what if I said that I didn't want to use my writing to make Rodrigo do anything anymore?"

"You will, though." Grammy's tone was horribly calm. "Because if you don't, he'll go right back to the same pointless cycle of heisting that he was in before, because that's all he knows."

"No, he won't. He's tried to stop before. He told me so. He just couldn't because I kept writing more blasted books. If I don't write anymore, he'll do better."

"Maybe. Or maybe losing you will teach him that trying to change the pattern doesn't work, and conning girls out of their heirlooms is the only thing he's good at. The only way you can know he's all right is to make it happen."

"You're sick," Latisha spat. "You and whatever creepy entity you rode in on."

"But you know I'm right."

Latisha didn't answer. In a flurry of motion, she fled the galley as quickly as she could without actually running, until she finally reached her cabin. Heedless of the gown she was still wearing—had the ball really only been hours ago?—she dropped heavily onto her cot, and curled up on her side, trying to breathe evenly.

She thought she might cry, but the tears wouldn't come.

She tried to imagine a scenario where none of what Grammy had said happened. She could meet Rodrigo early in the morning, and they could talk. She would confess everything and tell him that it didn't have to change anything—that she was still the same person he'd known, but she'd wanted to tell him the truth.

He would listen, and maybe be a little afraid and confused at first, but then say at the end, "I understand. Thank you for telling me. It'll be all right."

Latisha tried to imagine this, but no matter what she did or what words she imagined using, the Rodrigo in her mind only looked at her with fear, contempt, or anger. The image, clashing with the memory of how he'd looked at her earlier that night, was too painful, and she finally was forced to give up.

It was still dark when she finally got to her feet and began searching for her everyday clothes. Linn might still want the dress for something, or they could sell it. She changed clothes and shoved her hair back into the plain bun she was accustomed to. They'd gotten rid of the blouse and jeans she'd been wearing when she first arrived, but as it was, she settled for the first set of clothes they'd given her.

Those would probably be the easiest for them to spare.

It took a few minutes of hunting through the ship, but she was able to find paper and ink. It took a good deal longer to write out what she needed to say, but she made herself do it anyway.

If she was going to do this to him, Rodrigo deserved to know the truth. She didn't want him hunting all over the city for her, panicking and thinking she might be in trouble. Betrayal and an existential crisis would probably feel worse at the time, but it would give him more closure in the end.

Having left the letter on her cot where she knew the captain would find it, Latisha made her way up to the deck, passing Grammy going back to bed on the way. The older woman seemed to know what decision she'd reached and nodded to her without saying anything.

The sky was still dark, although it was looking a little pale off to the east, as if dawn wasn't far away.

She needed to hurry. Today of all days, Rodrigo was sure to be up early.

Resisting any feelings of foolishness, Latisha spoke into the night.

"I love Rodrigo, but he deserves better than I've given him, and so does this world. I need to go home to take care of that."

There wasn't an answer, and for a moment, nothing happened. Then a terrible sensation of falling overwhelmed her, and she cried out before she could help it—

—only to find herself on the rug of her office, back in her apartment.

Chapter 18

Rodrigo woke up slowly as the early morning light spread over his face, and for a moment, he couldn't immediately remember why he was so happy.

There had been a ball . . . and then they'd come back to the ship, he and Ellis . . . something had happened with Ellis. Something that had his insides feeling like they were made of warm, bright light before he even recalled the details.

Then it came—Ellis had kissed him. They'd had a fight, and he'd finally managed to tell her he loved her. It was far from the first time he'd said that to a woman, but this time was different because he'd meant it. He didn't plan on ever saying it to another woman, and he might actually be able to keep that internal promise this time.

She hadn't said the same to him, but the way she'd looked at him gave him hope that perhaps he wouldn't have to wait long to hear it.

With sudden energy, he sprang out of his bunk and began hunting for some clothes. Ellis had said she would meet him this morning before the crew got up, and they would talk and figure things out.

Clearly, some things would need to change around here. They'd need to do the heists differently, or maybe find a different line of work altogether—Rodrigo was not going to go around romancing random rich women while trying to court Ellis. A part of him wanted to drop the operation with Lady Jennifer, but they'd already put too much preparation into it to let it go.

Changing occupations had never worked out before, but everything had been different since Ellis came, so maybe this could be different too. Beyond that, he tried his best to imagine what might follow, but he had no clue whatsoever.

It was going to be an adventure, wooing a woman who he actually wanted to stay with.

Maybe he could ask Asad for advice, strange as the idea sounded. Asad had managed to maintain a healthy marriage with a strong, intelligent woman for a few years now—he probably had a few tips to pass on.

Emerging from his cabin, Rodrigo made his way to the galley and stuck his head in, but there was only Grammy rattling around making breakfast. Ellis wasn't on the deck, either. She probably hadn't gotten up yet and was still in her cabin. They had been out rather late last night, and she'd slept in after the last ball.

He approached her door and knocked quietly, not wanting to wake anyone else in the vicinity up. "Ellis? Are you awake yet?"

No reply. He gave it a few seconds, then tapped again, slightly louder. "Ellis! Best wake up if we want to hash things out before the whole crew's up."

Still no answer. Rodrigo knocked louder, and didn't hear so much as a half-awake mumble in response on the other side of the door. A chilly, paralyzing fear bloomed deep in his gut and seemed to spread through his body like smoke. Which was ridiculous because there was nothing to be even the slightest bit afraid of. He'd never tried to wake Ellis up before, and she was probably just a heavy sleeper.

All the reassurances and rationalizations his mind offered couldn't stop him from reaching out and opening the door the slightest crack, foolhardy as such an action would have been if Ellis was, in fact, there. Cautiously, and prepared to shut his eyes and bolt if the cabin's resident was anything less than fully clothed,

131

Rodrigo peered around the door into the dimly lit room.

She definitely wasn't up and about—the room was empty. The cot was too shadowed for him to make out anything properly.

Trying to suppress the undoubtedly foolish dread rising up inside him, Rodrigo opened the door fully, letting in more light, and stepped inside. Not only was the room empty, but the cot was unoccupied, and hadn't been slept in. The blanket was slightly ruffled, as though someone had lain on top of it at some point, but the bedding hadn't been disarranged enough for even the most peaceful sleeper.

He took all this in at a glance, and as he tried to come up with an explanation, he spotted the letter.

It had been left in the middle of the bed, folded in thirds so that no writing showed. Rodrigo stared at it for long moments, trying not to imagine all the things it might say. *Captain, last night was foolish, and I apologize. Unfortunately, I can't continue to work with a man whom I've . . . Darling, I couldn't sleep and I've started our walk early. Meet me at . . . Rodrigo, last night was a mistake. I can't believe I let myself forget how much I loathe you . . .*

This was ridiculous. He reached out and snatched up the paper, unfolding it determinedly and reading.

Rodrigo,

I have a confession to make. It's complicated, and it's going to hurt you, but it has to be this way. I'm so sorry.

I've led you to believe that I am Amora Ellis, a gentlewoman fallen on hard times, and that I knew nothing about any of you before I arrived on the Rake. None of that is true. The truth is that I am a writer, and, as insane as it sounds, I'm from a different world.

Not a different planet—a whole separate reality, if you can imagine it.

Where I'm from, I used to make a living writing romantic novels about a bold, swashbuckling captain who lives on a flying ship and seduces rich young women in order to steal from them with the help of his loyal crew. Sound familiar?

The novels were about you, Rodrigo, but I didn't know they were really happening, I swear.

I didn't like writing those novels, because I thought that the person I made you act like was the person you wanted to be. I thought you were naturally foolish and reckless and womanizing, when I was the one who made you be that way. You can imagine my dismay when I found myself inadvertently transported here.

But then something strange happened, even stranger than traveling from one world to another. I got to know you, and I learned to care for you, even if I didn't want to admit how much until last night. I thought perhaps I could stay here for the rest of my life and forget all about who I used to be. I would never have kissed you if I didn't think there was at least a possibility that we could make a life together. I want you to know that.

I thought I could stay, but something has reminded me that I could never be with you while living a lie. I know that once you know the truth you will probably see me differently, and that I would have had to leave anyway, so I have returned to my own world.

I will miss you, and I will miss the crew, but I will try to be happy.

I'll be all right; please don't worry about me.

What I want more than anything is for you to have what's best for you. I'm going to try and fix some of the things wrong with your world — the indifference of the grandfolk, the injustice so many people live with — but I won't make you do anything you wouldn't want to, I promise.

The cycle of heists will stop, as you've been wanting them to.

Grammy knows more about how all this happened than I do — she's tried to explain but I don't fully understand. Apparently there is a name for what I am — a scrivener. One who makes worlds out of written words. I've been told it's a gift, but it doesn't feel like one.

Anyway, talk to Grammy, she'll be able to explain, hopefully.

I will fix this, but I have to go. I'm so, so sorry.

She'd signed it scratchily, with multiple crossed-out attempts and childlike handwriting, as if she'd had to force the letters onto the page.

Love,

Latisha Robbins.

Rodrigo stared at the creased sheet of paper for longer than he knew, disbelieving. This was impossible. Surely this was a joke—some elaborate prank she'd set up for unfathomable reasons. She must be hiding somewhere on the ship or waiting for him out on the docks. She would tease him for being so gullible and he wouldn't be able to stay angry with her because at least she would be *there.*

The letter said to go talk to Grammy. She would tell him where Ellis had actually gone. She would tell him something.

Grammy was still in the galley, setting things out on the table for the upcoming breakfast. The utter normalcy of it snapped something in Rodrigo. If there was even the faintest possibility that the contents of this blasted letter were true, nothing should be continuing as normal. The sky should be dark and stormy and people should be shuddering and hiding under their blankets.

The older woman looked up calmly as he stormed in, having abandoned all pretense of stealth. "Morning, Captain," she said evenly. "Something I can help you with? If you're looking for Ellis, she doesn't work galley after her nights out."

"No, she doesn't," Rodrigo rejoined, low and dangerous. "According to this letter I found in her cabin, she doesn't work anywhere on this ship anymore. Apparently she talked to you just before making that decision—assuming this whole setup is real and not an elaborate hoax. So, tell me: does the word 'scrivener' mean anything to you?"

The look in Grammy's eyes, not remotely surprised but rather as if he'd just confirmed something, told him all he needed to know. "Ah. So, she went through with it, then."

It was not normally in Rodrigo's nature to speak aggressively towards women of advanced age, but today was not a normal day. He moved further into Grammy's space, a hint of snarl creeping into his voice. "What, exactly, did you have to do with that, then?" he demanded. "How long have you known that she wasn't from here and that she made us all up out of her own head? And you didn't think I deserved a warning? No 'Captain, sir, maybe don't become attached to this woman. She knows about every regrettable thing you've ever done and she made you do them'?"

Grammy merely regarded him solemnly. "If I had told you, would you have believed me? Or would you have thought I'd gone 'round the bend, and carried on just the same anyway?"

He wouldn't have believed her, and he knew it, but rather than admit it, he turned away to leave. He didn't want to have anything further explained to him, whether that was about what scriveners were or how Ell—Latisha had come and gone.

He certainly didn't want to know why or how this all was supposedly for the best.

Before he could get away, however, Grammy called after him, "She really did want what was best for you, even if it made her unhappy. She wouldn't have left if she didn't think it had to be done." Then, "I'm sorry. I'd hoped things would work out for the two of you."

Rodrigo didn't even dignify that with a response, moving almost blindly through the corridor and into the privacy of his cabin, slamming the door behind him more forcefully than he'd intended. He dropped onto the bunk, trying to find a place in his mind away from the maelstrom of painful, disjointed thoughts swirling through him. His eyes, flicking around the room, fell on the clothes from the previous night's ball, lying in a discarded heap on the floor, and his control cracked.

What had been going on in E—Latisha's mind these past weeks? Had she thought it amusing to toy with him like this? She'd described his previous romantic encounters; had she perhaps decided she wanted to partake in one herself? Had she endured his affections until she could make good on her escape once she'd found it too complicated to be with a man she'd imagined?

Oh, sweet smoking heavens above, she'd imagined him into existence. She'd imagined his whole world into existence, through

135

the simple act of writing a story. If her letter was to be believed, she'd had no idea. How could someone be that powerful and not know about it? How had she been able to pass for an ordinary person like anybody else around him?

There were little things, now that he thought about it, that might have warned him there was something off about her. The everyday kitchen devices, the weapons, and even the clothes had been strange to her when she first came, as if she'd known about them in theory but never had any practical experience with them.

When they'd explained to her how they made a living, she hadn't seemed surprised, but more like she'd always known. He should've guessed something was afoot, but he would never have guessed this.

She'd just been Amora Ellis. Just a person like they were people.

Aside from being a scrivener, she'd been quite an extraordinary person, in her own way. An amazing woman, and quite possibly the love of his miserable life, but not . . .

Oh. Wait a minute. He still loved her.

Even with what he knew, and what she'd done to him—both in the past and more recently—Latisha was still on some level the woman he'd come to know and deeply fallen for. He could see it in that letter, where her personality and turns of phrase were still present.

That was probably the most painful thought of all.

It meant there was no way she could love him, or that she knew him well at all. Latisha was surely intelligent enough to know that what was best for him was to have her by his side, always, and yet she had gone away instead. She'd promised to never make him do anything he didn't want to again, but was forcing him to live without her.

She had handed him this burden of knowledge and hadn't stayed to help him deal with it.

Rodrigo couldn't begrudge her wanting to leave, under the circumstances. He just wished she had told him this to his face.

When he knew the crew would be assembled in the galley, Rodrigo went out to face them and give them some version of the news. Best to get it over with all at once, rather than over and over again with each one.

"Where's Ellis?" Linn asked the moment he walked in. "She's usually up by now. I thought you two were going to—"

Right. Straight to the point it was. He cut her off before she could add any unnecessary, painful detail. "Ellis has found an opportunity for employment elsewhere. She had to be off early this morning but asked me to say goodbye to you all for her. She did promise she wouldn't let slip any details with regards to the heist, so you needn't worry about that."

There was no way he was going to tell them the full and complete truth. It was bad enough that he knew they'd all come into existence because of some piece of trashy fiction; he wouldn't burden anyone else with the revelation.

Asad and Linn looked distinctly confused and a little skeptical, like they knew there was more he wasn't telling them. Ruby was trying to hide a betrayed expression. Grammy sat regarding him with something painfully like sympathy, but he didn't want it.

Rationally, there was no reason for him to be angry at Grammy, but he had to be angry at somebody, and she was the only other one who knew any version of the truth.

"We are going to proceed with the heist," he went on. "It will be difficult, I know, since Ellis was to play such a large part in it, but Linn and I will come up with something in time for the planned-upon date."

If Latisha was going to start dictating their actions again, those plans might well be rendered moot, but in case she didn't, it would be a poor use of that freedom to sit around idly waiting to be stripped of agency. And regardless of broken hearts and sky-shattering revelations about the nature of his reality, his crew still needed to eat and stay flying, and it was still his responsibility to take care of them.

Quietly, and only to himself, he knew he needed the distraction if he was going to conceal from the others just how hard this had hit him, if he was going to maintain any illusion of still functioning.

Chapter 19

Latisha dug her fingers into the fabric of the rug, trying to ground herself in the feel of it.

She managed to get herself onto her knees and found herself staring at the contents of her office, something she'd probably seen a thousand times before but which now seemed too strange for words.

The colors looked all wrong—the rug she was clinging to was a few different shades of beige, the walls were a pale gray-green, and her desk was a sensible sepia. In the Rakish Heart world, everything had been full of vibrant, rich color, even the machines.

By comparison, the things around her seemed dull and undersaturated—the only objects that came close to looking right were the neatly lined-up novels on the shelf above her desk.

She didn't want to look at those.

She managed to get to her feet, only then realizing that she was still in her borrowed clothes. She would have expected the skirt, corset, and high-heeled boots to feel unnatural now that she was back in her proper world, but it was all still far more comfortable than appearances would suggest.

If anything, walking on the plush carpet and breathing in the once-familiar smell of her apartment, with not a trace of smoke in the air, was more disorienting.

The clock on her bedside table told her it was 4:13 in the morning. Latisha knew there were any number of things she should desperately want to do now that she was home, but she didn't care to try and remember any of them.

She had, very briefly, been unspeakably happy. She had found a place and people who felt like home, and she had chosen to throw it all away.

She didn't especially want to face any kind of reality right now.

She dropped face-down onto her neatly made, slightly dusty bed, and fell asleep almost immediately.

When she awoke, it was to the feeling of warm sunlight on her back. That wasn't right. Her closet-cabin didn't have a window, although they'd talked about cutting her one—

Everything came trickling back, and she remembered where she was. She rolled over and sat up, wincing as she remembered she'd slept in her corset.

With that twinge came the reminders of all the needs she'd forgotten when she first arrived—she was hungry, her clothes had grown stiff and uncomfortable, she'd never cleaned up after all that dancing a lifetime ago, and she'd been missing for who knew how long.

Clearly, this wasn't something where you returned the moment you'd left, or she would have come back in the late afternoon. Had she been gone here for as much time as had passed in the other world? How much time had that been, exactly?

Seized with a sudden need to act, Latisha stood and stripped off everything she was wearing. She dumped it in a corner before marching across the hall for her first real shower in at least several weeks.

This, she would freely admit, she had missed. Sponging off with a damp cloth and a basin, or in a metal tub of lukewarm water before and after a ball, just wasn't the same.

Freshly clad in jeans and an old band t-shirt, Latisha glanced at the clock—quarter to noon, close enough to lunch—and looked in the pantry for something canned. If she'd been gone long enough for her fridge to turn into a disaster area, she didn't want to witness it quite yet.

As the soup heated, she finally braced herself and went for her phone.

The date was April 13. She'd been gone for nearly two months—probably the same amount of time as she'd been in the *Rakish Heart* world (Rakeworld?), although she'd been starting to lose count of the weeks there outside of the countdown to May Day.

Clearly, she'd underestimated how much could happen in two months, as her phone was jammed with missed calls, texts, calendar alerts, and emails. A couple of the voicemails were from her mother, and a few were from acquaintances, but most were from her agent.

Right. She was supposed to have met Evie for lunch a few days after she'd vanished, and her radio silence following the missed appointment couldn't have helped with putting the woman's mind at ease.

Especially since—oh no, she'd had a draft due last week, hadn't she?

Latisha supposed she ought to panic, but there didn't seem to be much point, since if she were to have her way, the draft in question would never be finished anyway.

She cleared out her alerts, consumed the soup, and cleaned up the kitchen. Only then did she pick up the phone and dial.

Evie's bubbling voice filled her ear almost before the call rang once. "'Tisha! Oh, thank goodness. I can call off that PI now. Where have you been? I've been calling you and everything else I know how to do—it's like you vanished off the face of the earth!"

"Evie. Hi."

"Don't 'Evie. Hi,' me. What happened to you? Are you all right? Is the new book going to be finished on time?"

"It's a long story, yes, and I don't know. Look, I'm sorry to have worried you. If you want, I'll meet you tomorrow and explain, okay? Just thought I should let you know I was alive."

"Oh." Evie sounded slightly mollified. "All right then. Just as long as you don't stand me up again. I wasn't kidding about hiring a detective." With that, she hung up.

Latisha stared at the phone for a moment, then set it down and made herself walk into her office. She didn't think her trip would have affected a saved electronic document, but nothing about this scrivener business made sense, so it was better that she check now and get it over with.

Nothing had changed from the last time she'd touched the draft. It still left off just after Rodrigo's rescue of Lady Jennifer from a runaway carriage. None of the events of the past weeks were there —but she remembered them.

If she tried to continue the story from that point and wrote over the section of time she'd been present, would it retroactively change what had happened? Would Rodrigo and the others forget her? What would happen to her own memories of her stay there?

Perhaps it would be better for Rodrigo if she shifted his reality so he had never met her and gotten his heart broken, but she couldn't bring herself to do that. If she were honest with herself, she wasn't sure she would ever be able to directly write about him again, and she definitely wouldn't be able to write him in a heist.

She saved the document carefully and closed it, then spent the rest of the day working out a timeline for how long she'd spent in Rodrigo's world. As far as she could determine by that evening, she'd been there for just under eight weeks—the same amount of time as had passed in this world. There would only be seventeen days until the May Day ball for her and for them, which was a painfully short amount of time to prepare, work out a way to integrate Linn as Rodrigo's second, and change anything that needed changing due to Latisha's absence.

Should she have stayed until the heist was over, to avoid causing so much trouble, or was it better to have broken off cleanly instead of hiding a guilty secret for weeks?

Neither option seemed satisfactory since what she really wanted was to not have had to leave at all.

Evie met her for lunch at the quasi-Italian bistro they usually favored. Latisha hadn't expected the occasion to be especially pleasant, but there was no getting out of it, and in any case, the bistro boasted an unusually good gelato. She mentally added 'ice cream' to the list of things she hadn't had since Before.

It was easier to think about the whole experience if she only referred to it by prepositions: there had been a Before, when she had been content, and a During, when she had been frustrated and then suddenly happy, and now there was After.

After the *Rake*, after learning to fight with a sword, after Rodrigo—Latisha now wondered if she could live the whole rest of her life, make a million dollars, write the book she'd always wanted to write, marry a wonderful man, and travel the world, and all of it would still feel like one great big After.

"'Tisha!" Evie greeted her in a blizzard of powder pink fluff and teased blonde curls, with a squeal and a tight hug that belied what was technically a professional relationship. "Come on, come on, sit down. Tell me all about it."

Latisha had already decided that she was going to lie. Someday, she might tell someone the truth, but that someone would never be Evie. "There's not much to tell, really. I . . . well, I suppose I sort of had a breakdown. Stress, you know. I had to get away, so I went out to this retreat place my, um, second cousin owns."

Evie harrumphed slightly. "Well, I suppose that means those cops I talked to were right. They dragged their feet like you wouldn't believe when I reported you missing—kept on saying there was no sign of a struggle, so I finally ditched them and got Detective Nolan on the case."

Latisha couldn't quite meet her eyes. "I'm . . . sorry. I didn't want to tell anybody that I was feeling so bad, and I didn't have cell coverage out there—it was all very spur-of-the-moment. But I should've given you some notice."

143

"Aw, don't worry about it." Evie leaned across the table, taking Latisha's hand with a sweet, earnest, polished smile. "Stress can be so awful sometimes. Did you at least have a good time?"

"It was all right. A little rustic, but that was kind of what I needed." A small smile crept onto Latisha's face as she considered mixing in a little of the truth. "I . . . met this man there."

"Oh, 'Tisha, you never!"

"I did. But I had to leave him. There was no way it could last."

"Aw, you poor thing. Just like one of those heroines in your books." Evie patted her hand, then perked up. "Speaking of which, when can you have the next one drafted? I've been stalling the publishing house until I could find you, but they're starting to tap their feet a little bit."

"Um, about that." Latisha pulled her hands away. "Evie, I've been thinking about not doing any more installments on the Rakish Heart series. I . . . I just can't keep doing this. I can live on the royalties from the books that are already out, or find something else to do, or . . . I don't know. But I want to stop."

Evie's head tilted to one side, as if she hadn't heard correctly. "Excuse me?"

"I want to stop writing the Rakish Heart novels."

"Like, stop entirely?"

"Yes. I don't think I can even finish the one I was working on. I had this . . . revelation, I guess you could say, while I was gone, and I know what I want for my life, and it doesn't involve me writing mind-numbing drivel for lonely anachronists to drool over. I'm done." That was actually all pretty much the truth. Just not quite in the right order, and with some important pieces taken out.

Evie looked like she was scrambling for a counterargument, but Latisha wasn't worried. She'd done a little research since getting back and knew that the publishers couldn't, at this stage, require her to deliver *Pride and Persuasion*. They also couldn't hire someone else to ghostwrite the series—she didn't think it would affect the world if they did, any more than the fan fiction she knew of had—but it was better to be sure.

"But what are you gonna do, then?" Evie finally asked. "Write something else? You could've warned me I was going to lose my biggest client, you know."

"No writing, not for . . . a while." Maybe if she could figure out a way to write without scrivening a new world, she would consider it. But for the time being . . . "Right now, I just want to settle back in."

Chapter 20

For the first few days after Ellis—Latisha's vanishing, Rodrigo was on tenterhooks, sure that at any moment he would find himself doing something ridiculous against his will as he usually did this close to the denouement of a heist.

The anticipation would have driven him half-mad anyway but knowing what such an event would mean—that the woman he'd given his heart to was knowingly treating him like a puppet—made the uncertain waiting worse.

But no such thing happened, and it kept on not happening, so Rodrigo finally decided that he might as well plan for the heist under the assumption that he would be in full control of his actions.

They'd had almost everything figured out before El—Latisha left, but now certain things would have to be revised to work around her absence. Linn wanted to find some way to accompany him despite clearly not being the person he'd previously been attending with and had suggested being introduced as his cousin, though that would stretch believability at best.

But in the end, Rodrigo convinced her that it would be simpler if he went in on his own. It might even be an improvement, he argued: there would be no fiancée or other plus-one for him to pretend to evade in order to slip away to Lady Jennifer's room.

And so, by the time May Day approached, the plan was more or less solidified, and not all that different from his usual procedure.

146

He would arrive at the ball, dance with Lady Jennifer and sweep her off her feet, then eventually persuade her that they should adjourn to her bedroom. There, he would keep up a pretense of seduction until she had unlocked her private safe to put away her jewelry, at which point he'd knock her out with certain pressure points in the neck. He would then be free and clear to empty out the safe and escape out the window, where Asad would have a rope ladder from the *Rake* waiting for him.

That, at least, was what they thought he would be doing. Rodrigo had his own ideas in mind, but reasoned that if he were to disclose them, Linn would try to talk him out of it. Better to just go ahead with it and apologize afterward if necessary.

Days turned into weeks, and he kept busy. He didn't catch himself starting towards the weapons cupboard at the time of day when he should have been sparring with E—*Latisha*, and he didn't think about how no one had started using the closet-turned-cabin for storage again or how Linn hadn't taken her donated clothes back, and he didn't keep letting his eyes drift toward the empty place next to Grammy at meals. He didn't waste time wondering what that other world was like, and about all the ways it might be better than his own.

Or if he did do any of these things, he would certainly never have admitted to them.

And then it was May Day.

He arrived on the deck to find Linn and Asad with their heads together over a city map, and when Linn looked up at his approach, she frowned.

"I thought you were going to wear green," she commented.

Technically, that would have been the better course of action—Lady Jennifer was known for always wearing green, and since he was attending her ball ostensibly to woo her, with no fiancée in tow this time, he should be at least attempting to follow her color scheme. But the crimson waistcoat and cravat he'd donned were what he'd originally been slated to wear, to match the gown planned for Latisha, and he found he was not especially inclined to alter that portion of the plan.

"Anything green I own is in the laundry sack," he shrugged. It wasn't an untrue answer—he'd purposely put it all there himself—but that wasn't relevant information.

Linn gave him a long, thoughtful look, but didn't say anything besides, "Don't do anything reckless."

Given what he had planned for the rest of the night, Rodrigo chose to forgo a verbal response, instead shooting her a cocky half-grin as he crossed to the rope ladder and the start of the most important heist of his career.

Under optimal circumstances, Rodrigo would have preferred to not make more than a few minutes' appearance at the Bartram May Day ball, if that. But because Linn and Asad were under the impression that he would need sufficient time to romance their mark, he had no choice but to participate in the event as normal until closer to when his means of escape would arrive.

That was probably just as well, since he had no sooner set foot in the ballroom than he spotted Lady Jennifer, who was unmistakably headed his way. Her eyes were sharp and gleaming and her smile predatory in ways he had never noticed before.

He couldn't decide whether this was a new expression for her or whether he'd simply been too preoccupied in the past to pick up on it, but before he could think on it further, she had reached him.

"Señor del Rey," she greeted him, extending her hand. He took it and bowed automatically. "No charming fiancée this evening?"

"She is indisposed," he recited smoothly, "but she sends her best."

"Oh, I am sure." Lady Jennifer looked like a cat that had seized upon the fattest mouse in the room. Under other circumstances, he might have assumed that this was triumph in her having secured his undivided attention, but he couldn't help but suspect that there was something else at work. What interest she'd shown in him before had always been more coy and discreet—always something that could be plausibly denied in the face of gossip.

This was entirely different, and he wasn't sure if he trusted it.

Then again, the change could simply be because he was unaccompanied, and she had less reason to hide. Indeed, she went on to almost purr, "In that case, I suppose I can claim all your dances without inviting the shrieking of a harpy on either of us."

He flashed a smile of agreement at that and followed the clear suggestion to lead her into the first set, but couldn't quite ignore the whisper in his mind, suspiciously like Latisha's, that pointed out *there's something not right here. She's trying to put you at ease. You're not the only one who knows how to play this game . . .*

According to the enormous clock built into one wall, he had an hour remaining before the *Rake* would be in position to give him an exit. He could spend perhaps a quarter of that time on the theft itself without risking being caught. That left three-quarters of an hour to endure this and remain above suspicion while keeping Lady Jennifer happy.

He could manage that. After all, if he had his way, after tonight he would never have to infiltrate a party of the grandfolk again.

The music changed to a waltz—the same tune, he realized, that he'd last danced to with Latisha. If he let his eyes flick away from his real partner, he could almost imagine that it was her he was dancing with now. He could imagine all too clearly the way it would have been without that letter: Ellis, resplendent in the crimson gown Linn had altered for her, trying to still pretend to hate him even though they would both have known better. Or perhaps, if she had found some way to tell him the whole truth and still stay, they could still have done this—infiltrated the ball and danced for the fun of it and gone on to rob Lady Jennifer blind, her scrivener's knowledge giving them an insurmountable advantage.

But he couldn't fool himself for long. Lady Jennifer moved in a completely different way, like she was trying too hard to draw passion out of him. It had never occurred to Latisha to do any such thing, and she had never needed to anyway.

Lady Jennifer seemed to think she had succeeded, though, because as the dance came to an end, instead of curtsying as was typically called for, she stepped closer into his space, pressing herself nearly flush with him. She seized the lapels of his jacket and pulled him down into a kiss.

For one horrifying moment, he thought that perhaps this was Latisha's doing—that she had taken up the narrative of his life again—but he felt none of the complacent acceptance that characterized those times, and he was all too familiar with the languorous, pliant way that marks would kiss him under such circumstances. What Lady Jennifer was doing was completely different; it was hard and fast and a little desperate, trying to work his mouth open almost immediately despite the fact that they were in public.

Perhaps he should have gone along with it. It was the perfect opportunity to engage the plan as Linn and Asad knew it, if a little early in coming—but all he could think about was how Latisha had kissed him, equally unexpected but so much more welcome. That kiss had spoken of the hesitancy and desire seeming to war within her, and he found he could not stand this other, lesser touch a moment more.

With effort, he broke away, doing his best to breathe normally and not bothering to hide the confusion on his face.

"Forgive me, my lady," he said, as soon as he could manage coherent speech, "it seems we have made a spectacle of ourselves. I must take my leave."

He fled as quickly as was possible without looking like he was fleeing, and did not look back at the wide-eyed, gossiping guests or let himself think until he had made it to a different, deserted part of the house.

He would have to go for it now, he decided once he got his wits back. It was too early, but he could wait on the roof with his ill-gotten goods. That was preferable to staying any longer where Lady Jennifer and the inexplicable strangeness that had come over her could find him.

A quick glance around and he had his bearings—Latisha had drawn up remarkably detailed floor plans during their plotting sessions, plans that he now knew could not have come entirely from whatever scouting she'd done during their previous visit. He could easily make it to Lady Jennifer's bedchamber from here without crossing paths with any servants.

A few turns, a couple of flights of stairs, and a quick walk down a corridor, and he had found it. The room was unquestionably the right one: aside from the prevailingly green color scheme, he recognized the cosmetics on the vanity and a couple of lesser trinkets lying on a table as hers.

The plan was supposed to be for Lady Jennifer to unwittingly give him access to the safe with her more valuable jewels, including the Star of Atlantis that was ostensibly his target, but since he knew where the safe was and roughly how to crack it, there was no particular need for her presence, besides saving him time.

Rodrigo found himself grinning as he opened the wall paneling and set to work on the locks. This was the kind of work he'd originally dreamed of doing, back when he and Linn were young and scraping by—daring adventure, stealing jewels, but not hearts that he didn't want anyway. He wondered idly whether that had been the kind of story Latisha had originally meant to write for him—otherwise, why would he have ever been anything but the rake he'd shifted into?

If she'd found a way to tell him the truth, perhaps he could have asked her why she'd chosen to write what she did when she seemed to hate it so and whether any of the hints she'd dropped about her life had basis in reality.

With an enormously satisfying clunk, the safe unlocked and swung open. Rodrigo suppressed a laugh of triumph—he'd done it!

He was capable of doing this, being the man he'd once dreamed of becoming. He quickly scooped up the Star of Atlantis, set in gold as an ornate necklace, and deposited it in a jacket pocket.

Technically, his work here was done, but he pulled out the rest of the contents in double handfuls and pocketed them as well. Regardless of his usual habits, it would be foolish to leave such wealth just sitting there when he had access to it. It was the work of moments to clear out the safe, and then to move around the rest of the room, gathering anything that looked sellable and that would fit in his pockets.

Perhaps with a haul like this, he could make up for the income Linn hadn't been able to bring in with her injury, and even keep them flying while they figured out something new to do.

Latisha might not still be here for him to be faithful to, but given his success so far tonight, she did seem to be done directing his life, and—barring interference—he was never going to kiss or caress a woman as part of a con again.

He finished with the room and was only a few steps from the window when a quiet 'ahem' behind him made him freeze.

It was Lady Jennifer. Of course.

She stood in the doorway, expression serene, not seeming at all disquieted or even surprised to find him looting her bedroom.

"Ah, Captain," she said, sweet as poison. "How kind of you to let yourself be caught red-handed after all. When you ran away earlier, I was afraid you'd lost your nerve."

This was too many changes in demeanor in one night for Rodrigo to keep up with. "What?" he asked, the question encompassing several points of confusion at once.

"You really aren't as clever as the rumors make you out to be," Lady Jennifer observed, head tilting to one side. "I would have thought you'd do your research, but evidently not, or you would have realized that House Bartram is dipping ever closer to poverty. Most of our wealth is tied up in this house and the heirlooms in your pockets—things not so easy to sell and still maintain one's pride. So, imagine my delight when you came poking around—a wanted thief with such a high reward for your arrest. One hundred thousand, did you know? It made enduring your attentions, distracted as they were, a great deal easier to bear, let me tell you, although I fear I shall have to wash my mouth out to prevent contracting disease, after trying to stall you earlier."

A rush of rhythmic, running footsteps, and Lady Jennifer stepped back to allow half a dozen police, armed with rifles, to rush into the room.

Rodrigo raised his hands slightly, fairly sure they wouldn't shoot him right there but unwilling to take chances, and spotted, out of the corner of his eye, movement outside the window.

Asad, blessedly, had arrived early and gotten the rope ladder in place.

If he were lucky, he could sprint those last few steps to the window, crash through, catch hold, and escape—but the police were armed and a few were noticeably twitchy. They would likely shoot him before he could get far, and he would fall either to the floor or into the street, not doing anyone any good. There was another option, though . . .

Slowly, carefully, he started to shrug his jacket off his shoulders, to work his arms out of the sleeves. "Why didn't you have me seized when I first met you, then?" he inquired, hoping the ill-gotten valuables in his pockets weren't clinking too audibly. "If you knew who I was right away." He knew why she hadn't at their initial meetings—Latisha would have prevented her—but he was curious about the later occasions.

Lady Jennifer huffed. "The law in this city fines anyone who falsely reports a crime—it was an unlikely risk, since you were already wanted, but one I couldn't take with my house's finances in the state they were. But I ended up getting some rather unlikely assistance—I believe you're familiar with a Floriane Bonheur? Evidently, she likes you even less than I do. I got the impression she was rather envious of your Miss Ellis."

Rodrigo closed his eyes briefly and sighed. He probably should have known he hadn't heard the last of Floriane. For a moment, he spared a thought to wonder whether she would have come after him much sooner if it hadn't been for Latisha's writing. "I'm surprised she's not here to gloat," he commented, trying to keep his voice light and casual.

"Oh, she's already in custody—she quite neatly confessed to several unsolved burglaries and acts of piracy in the process of implicating you. Between the two of you, my house's finances should be looking up nicely. I would have thought to receive another ten thousand recompense for assault upon a lady's person, but you've been downright shy all evening. I suppose it's no matter."

"Sorry to disappoint," Rodrigo said, deadpan, and the jacket was loose enough now that he could shrug it off entirely, catch its weight in one hand, and whirl around to smash out the window glass.

Half a dozen rifles cocked behind him, but he hurled the jacket out and away, holding his breath, and it landed perfectly over one of the ladder rungs, only dropping a few rings and hairpins in its flight. He caught a glimpse of Linn's face peering over the railing and gestured wildly to *go, go now* before stumbling back to face six flustered police and Lady Jennifer's icy, furious gaze.

"Rodrigo Antúnez," the apparent leader of the police said finally, "you are under arrest for multiple counts of theft, breaking and entering, fraud, and obstruction of justice. I advise you to come quietly and not try any further funny business, or it will go a great deal harder for you."

Another of them moved to clap heavy iron manacles onto Rodrigo's wrists, and he let the man, unable to help the grin spreading onto his face, or the laughter that threatened to well up out of him. Even Lady Jennifer's hateful stare and the constables' hands pulling a few lone trinkets out of his trouser pockets couldn't dampen his mood.

"I can only hope," Lady Jennifer said coldly, "that you can remain this merry over having stripped me of my valuables when you are thrown into Caderousse for the rest of your days—short may they be."

That last part was a sentiment all too likely to come true—Caderousse Prison, the usual destination for criminals of Rodrigo's type, was known for its miserable conditions and the short lifespans of its inmates. Perhaps this should have filled him with trepidation or depression, but instead, all Rodrigo could do was laugh, head thrown back.

Still chuckling, he bent down to speak into Lady Jennifer's ear as he was hauled past her. "You don't understand," he murmured. "I won. I will always have won."

It wasn't because he'd managed to get the take to his crew—not even remotely. If he was being taken away to prison, it proved beyond a doubt that Latisha was no longer attempting to write out his life. He might not have known her fully, but he knew her at least that well—she would never have chosen this ending for him.

She had given him his life to do with as he chose, and that meant that, in the ways that mattered, she really was the woman he'd come to love after all. He might die in prison, but he would be freer than he'd ever been.

And Latisha would never have to know.

She could live out her days in that mysterious world of hers, no doubt believing that he was still having adventures and getting himself into mischief for years to come. Believing, but never bringing that imagination to bear on his reality.

Rodrigo couldn't keep from laughing all the way to the cell they finally threw him into.

Chapter 21

Latisha had known it would be hard to come back to what most people would call the real world. She had expected, though, that it would get somewhat easier after a short adjustment period.

It didn't.

It had been over a fortnight since her return, and she still couldn't shake the sense that she was in the wrong place and that she didn't fit in this reality. She kept waking up hours before she had to, in her too-soft, too-wide bed, and found herself unable to get back to sleep because there was too much light coming in through the blinds in her room, even in early spring.

Clothes that should have been comfortable seemed ill-fitting to the point of distraction—t-shirts were too loose without a corset, and jeans felt constricting now that she'd gotten used to skirts. She couldn't sleep to modern city noise anymore, and had finally tracked down an audio file of engines running that she could loop at night.

More than once in the first few days, she'd gone to make one of Grammy's recipes out of habit and been stymied by a pantry full of canned and microwavable goods; she'd finally gone and bought the ingredients she needed and spent a quarter hour crying into the resulting stew. Most of the clothes she'd borrowed—stolen?— stayed buried at the back of her closet, but she wore the boots everywhere. They were the only thing that felt right anymore.

She told herself several times a day that the wrongness she felt was only from being in a different place, and not from missing her crew or being lonely without Rodrigo. But she couldn't stop thinking she saw the back of Asad's head or a flash of Ruby's face in crowds, and her pillows had teeth marks from the times she'd screamed into them when the lack of Rodrigo's warm voice and sideways smiles hurt too much to bear.

Not long after the lunch with Evie, she'd called her mother, bracing herself for a verbal torrent of worry and scolding. No such thing had occurred. None of her family had even known she was missing.

Evie didn't know them and either hadn't been able to or hadn't thought to contact them. Latisha called infrequently enough, what with their opinions of what she did for a living, that a six-week radio silence hadn't even been noticed—her mother was more surprised that she'd called when she did.

Perhaps it should have been a relief, but it mostly just felt like a mocking reminder of all the reasons she'd had to stay in the Rakeworld, as she'd settled on calling it.

She'd had just the one reason to come back—to fix her world and Rodrigo's life—but she hadn't written a word since returning. She'd tried different places, different formats, every trick the internet had to offer, but none of it worked.

Before, she'd been able to pound out a few thousand words in a sitting without thinking—it went better if she didn't think. But now, she was all too aware that her words would affect the lives of real people she cared about. Even if she confined herself to paragraphs of info-dumping, there was no clever life hack out there for dealing with that knowledge.

Then she woke up one morning and realized it was May 1, the day the heist had been meant to happen.

She needed to quit stalling and make the changes that had to be made before anything else could go wrong. So, once she'd dragged herself out of bed and fought through the haze of procrastination, she spread out several sheets of printer paper on the dining room table and went to work with a pencil, brainstorming.

It's just brainstorming, she insisted to herself. *It's not anything deliberate or permanent. Not yet.*

If she forced herself to believe that then it would probably stay true.

In a long, uneven column, she listed out all the things she could remember about the Rakeworld, both that she'd seen and that she could recall from what she'd written before. Every point was something that was wrong, harmful, or in need of excision.

The treatment of automata. The Sourcers, and the conditions in the factories they worked for. The slums that Rodrigo and Linn had grown up in and fought to escape. The pettiness and indifference of the grandfolk. The laws that made no sense and the deadly prisons that awaited those caught breaking them. And more, so many more.

She stared at the list, wondering where to start. She could just sit down and write a few sentences that made all these things go away. She could add a note about Floriane finally being arrested and not being able to bother Rodrigo again. That would almost definitely work, and it had the benefit of her only having to spend the bare minimum of time dealing with it.

But part of her recoiled at the idea. As effective as it might be, she would be making these changes without any in-world rhyme or reason, confusing everyone and creating chaos—and who knew what would happen in the aftermath? She could end up with something that was worse than she started with, and never know it.

Although, if I mess things up worse than they were before, Demodocus might pull me back—

Her heart leapt at that prospect, but she sternly reminded herself that she needed to avoid that scenario. Leaving Rodrigo had been hard enough the one time.

In that case, it seemed she had no choice but to work her desired changes in more slowly. She could probably do that in several pages of notes, without having to make it into a story per se, but it would take longer—a lot longer in the Rakeworld, because full social transformation was something that would take years, maybe even generations.

The factories were probably the only thing that she could do anything about right away, and even that was stretching the definition of 'right away'.

She still worked at it restlessly for several hours, plotting and pondering and jotting down purposely fragmented notes, trying to work out how it could all be done. Unfortunately, the more it came together, the more another issue began to creep into her awareness, one that was more difficult to shake.

If she had the power to change the Rakeworld like this, why not use that power to completely eliminate the social injustices she was concerned about? Why not simply retcon her old notes and make it so the unfair laws and the class divisions never existed? It would be the most effective way to make sure nobody was suffering because of her.

It was almost definitely the best way to handle, for example, Asad's situation—she could make it so that Vernes and other automata were free citizens from the beginning, not bound by purchased contracts to terrible people.

But then, why would anybody have invented automata unless they stood to gain from it?

More to the point, without that pervasive greed, Asad might have never ended up on the *Rake*. And he had to be there— partially because he'd been indispensable in several of the crew's plot points, but mostly because he was a *person* and had a life and people who loved him on the *Rake*, and that shouldn't be erased because she was struggling with her mistakes.

She tried to shake away the thought and carry on, but it wouldn't be shaken, and neither would the realizations that trailed after it: automata might not exist without greed, but *Rodrigo* wouldn't exist, at least not in the way she knew him, without a world where teeming slums and extravagant grandfolk and unjust laws did not exist. He had been shaped by poverty, unfairness, and a criminal overworld, and so had Linn, and Ruby, and Grammy. Asad existed because of a world of terrible working conditions where automata had been made to fill in the gap. They had only come together because of the ways their world was broken.

Perhaps she should have realized before, since practically the first thing anyone had told her about writing was that stories had to have conflict to function. She'd been so caught up, though, in the wonder and horror of her world and characters being real that she'd forgotten that what had made them real was a story. Without conflict, without imperfections, they would never have come to life at all.

And perhaps she could try to turn her world into a utopia, and perhaps it would even work. But while she might have brought the Rakeworld into existence, she would do a terrible job as its god. Her power was finite and imprecise, and her knowledge ultimately incomplete. She would never be able to make everything perfect.

She was all too liable to make things worse if she tried.

But it was just possible that if she were there in person, she could find smaller ways to make some things better.

She looked up from her mess of notes and stared at the wall clock. It was still a couple of hours shy of midnight. Time was running the same way in the Rakeworld as it did in the "real" world, more or less, so Rodrigo might still be at the Bartram house, with the night still young.

She couldn't bring herself to write the heist, not even to assure herself that Rodrigo was safe, but she could go back and protect him.

Could she go back, though? Grammy—Demodocus had sent her to her own world, to write things better . . .

Wait, though.

Grammy hadn't actually said she *had* to do that. She'd said Latisha *could,* and that she shouldn't let Rodrigo court her without telling him the truth. Latisha had then made her own choice about that.

But more than that, Grammy had said emotional connections—like love—could pull a scrivener between worlds without Demodocus' intervention.

Even as she thought about it, Latisha could feel that bond, growing stronger the more she focused on it. It was almost ready to tug her through whatever separated realities.

Maybe if she went back, Rodrigo would hate her or want her gone now that he knew the truth. If he did, then she would leave once the heist was done—once she knew he was all right.

The Rakeworld was a lot bigger than one ship and one city, and she should be able to find a place for herself in it. She'd still be heartbroken, but at least she'd be somewhere where she could breathe.

Latisha looked again at the list of impossible goals she'd tried to set for herself. She glanced around her apartment with all its modern conveniences and no life whatsoever. Then she grabbed a fresh sheet of paper and started to write—nothing world-changing, just a letter. When it was finished, she taped it up where it would be the first thing anyone saw if they came in the front door.

If you're looking for me, it said, *I'm quite all right, but I won't be coming back. I also won't be reachable for the foreseeable future. Evie, I'm sorry if this causes you concern, but please don't worry, and tell my family not to worry if you hear from them. I will be just fine.*

She got rid of her mess of brainstorming, headed into the office, and printed out the chapters she'd written of *Pride and Persuasion* before her escapade, then found the notes she had stored on her computer, printed them, and wiped everything.

Since she wasn't sure just what the threshold for reality was with this scrivening business, it was better to be safe than sorry.

The printouts and her old worldbuilding notebooks went in a

lockbox for safekeeping, but the novels with the cover art that barely resembled Rodrigo stayed where they were. She dug out the clothes she'd buried in the back of the closet and put them on, then pulled back her hair for good measure.

Only then, in the small hours of the morning, did she secure the lockbox under her arm and let herself give in, falling out of the world she'd been born in and into the one she'd made for herself.

She was in free fall for only for a moment as smoky-smelling wind lashed at her, before she landed hard on her hands and knees on a blessedly familiar wooden surface. The lockbox clunked onto the deck beside her, and then there were running footsteps coming closer, but Latisha ignored it all for a moment while she got her breath back, grinning at the planks under her.

She laughed, giddy and delighted, and only barely resisted the urge to kiss the deck. She was back on the *Rake*.

She was back in the world where she belonged. Everything else was details.

Long, dark leather boots appeared in her peripheral vision, and Linn gripped her arm and hauled her to her feet. "Ellis! What's going on, how did you—"

Latisha threw her arms around the other woman, cutting her off. "Linn! It's so good to see you. Where is everyone? Is the heist over yet?"

Linn extricated herself from the embrace, a grim look on her face. "The heist was this past night."

Relief rushed through her. "Oh, good, you all made it then." In her absence, Rodrigo would probably have taken Linn with him as his second, and if she was here, Rodrigo must be as well. Linn wouldn't have run for it and left him behind. "I'm so sorry I left you all in the lurch. Where's Rodrigo? I need to tell him—"

"He's in Caderousse."

Those three words smacked any trace of delight or giddiness out of her. "What? But—but with the plan we were working on, it should have been safer—and he should have had you with him, and you're better than I am . . . "

"He didn't take me with him," Linn snapped. "He said he'd be fine on his own, and then he went with a different plan that didn't involve seducing the mark—I can only imagine because of some clinging loyalty to you. But Lady Jennifer had made him anyway. The whole thing was a trap. He got us the take, and more besides, but they arrested him. He would've been taken to Caderousse."

Latisha fought down the horror rising in her. Caderousse Prison was a byword among skydwellers—a maze of open-air cages, constantly hovering over the sea. It was where the law sent people instead of executing them. Being sent there might not be an official death penalty, but the inmates of Caderousse typically died from exposure within the first several weeks of imprisonment, or if not from that, then from the irregular meals and frequent beatings from the guards.

No wonder Linn looked like she wanted to punch her. There was a pretty clear, and perhaps not all that inaccurate, line of blame to be drawn from Latisha's sudden disappearance to Rodrigo's going off-script and getting caught because of it.

Perhaps, Latisha thought sickly, he'd even wanted to be arrested, due to some kind of existential despair after what she'd revealed to him about the nature of his reality. And how much had he told the others about that revelation, anyway?

Judging by the accusations Linn hadn't hurled her way, she supposed he must not have told them much, if anything. So how had he explained her disappearance, besides the truth?

She needed to be able to ask him herself. She had come back prepared to deal with his rejection, but not to let him rot in jail.

"I—I'm so sorry, I didn't—if I'd known, I would've —" she attempted, but anything she could think of to say sounded useless. "What are you going to do? You must have a plan. What can I do to help?"

Linn looked at her like she was insane. "Do you think if there were anything we could do, we wouldn't already be doing it? That I haven't been racking my brain since I realized he'd been arrested, trying to come up with a solution? There is no plan. None whatsoever. Not for breaking Rodrigo out, not for how we're going to survive now, nothing." Her face twisted like she was trying not to cry, and Latisha remembered with a pang in her chest that this woman had been Rodrigo's closest friend since they were children, and that she was essentially already mourning him. "He loved you—did you know that?—and now he's as good as dead, and I would hate you for it if it wouldn't have happened sooner or later with or without your vanishing act."

Latisha wanted to comfort her but doing that would mean agreeing with her that Rodrigo was past saving, and she couldn't let herself do that. Instead, she kept trying frantically to think of a solution.

Her scrivener powers, even if she hadn't already decided to leave them alone, wouldn't do any good in this situation. Erasing Caderousse from the present would set free a small but significant population of violent criminals who did need to be contained somewhere.

Erasing it from the past would have worse consequences: Linn's father had been sent to Caderousse, leaving room for the abusive stepfather who'd eventually driven her to run away with Rodrigo in the first place. And crafting a narrative where the prison was reformed or shut down more organically would take months or longer in-world, and that was time Rodrigo didn't have.

She was going to have to take care of this from right where she was, with no more hopping back and forth between worlds. But that didn't mean she didn't have certain advantages she could use.

Behind Linn, she could see Grammy hauling herself up the ladder onto the deck, and locked eyes with her just briefly. The older woman didn't greet her, or express any surprise to see her back, just nodded like she'd suspected this would happen all along.

Bending down, Latisha scooped up the lockbox from where it

had fallen on the deck. "Linn," she said firmly, "he's not dead. Not yet. And we don't have to give up on him. I can get him out, I'm almost positive. I just need some help."

Linn looked at her incredulously—but also with just a tiny glimmer of hope in her eyes, and that was all Latisha needed. "What are you talking about?"

Latisha tapped the box full of the notes that made up the fragile bones of this world—including the pages where she'd once detailed the precise workings of Caderousse Prison. "I can't explain all of it right now, but I can get into that place and bring him out with me—without putting anyone else in danger. We don't have to lose anybody today. But you have to trust me."

It was, in all honesty, not the best or most logical argument Latisha could have made. But Linn, who had followed Rodrigo into and out of far too many crazy, impossible schemes, just looked at her for a long moment, and then nodded.

"Let me get the rest of the crew."

Chapter 22

For as long as he could remember, Rodrigo had heard horror stories about Caderousse.

In the slums where he'd grown up, everyone had talked about how exposed the cells were, how they little better than lattices of steel bars above, below, and on all sides. The skydwellers he'd become acquainted with later had spoken darkly about the loss of autonomy the prisoners were subjected to, locked up and at the whims of someone else's routine. A few more bigoted types had spat to the side when they muttered over how dehumanizing it was to only have automata guarding the place, with their rigid adherence to protocol and—allegedly—no human sympathy.

Rodrigo found that none of those factors were really as terrible as he'd been led to believe. The higher altitude and open air were a relief—those things had always felt like freedom to him, even if the wind was colder here and carried the salty ocean spray with it. The loss of autonomy wasn't so bad either—he knew all too well what true lack of independence felt like, and this simply didn't compare. And he thought he might actually prefer automaton guards: any guards would likely beat him because that was what happened in Caderousse, but while humans would be more random, these ones, of a less sentient security line called Burroughs, would probably stick to some sort of pattern that he could eventually puzzle out to better brace himself.

The worst part, and something that no one had warned him

about, however, was the worry for his crew. Financially, they should be all right—what he'd stolen from Lady Jennifer should keep them solvent for some time . . . and it turned out that Linn and Asad were the ones contributing most to the ship's coffers, anyway.

What caused him more concern was the possibility that they might decide to do something foolish like trying to break him out. He would have liked to think that they all had more common sense than to attempt any such thing, but considering the number of half-baked plans they'd followed him into over the years—Latisha's influence notwithstanding—he found he wasn't quite so confident.

After all, they'd always gotten away with those half-baked plans before. Hopefully, Linn's earlier injury and his own capture would give them a hint that whatever safety net they'd had before—Latisha's safety net—was no longer in effect.

True, their being sensible would mean that he would die here, but that seemed far more nebulous and less horrifying than the possibility of one or more of his crew suffering some terrible fate in a fruitless prison break.

He leaned back against one of the walls of his cage, trying to ignore the desiccating skeleton behind him, and let his eyes wander over the structure of the prison at large.

Caderousse was built on a three-dimensional grid of steel catwalks and ladders, ringed by black gasbags that kept it airborne and more or less in one place, and whose cabins served as quarters for the guards and processing centers for new prisoners. There was no real cover anywhere—perhaps a few odd corners that would protect someone from gunfire, but certainly nowhere that someone could be completely unseen.

In short, it was an absolute deathtrap.

He'd thought to entertain himself with plotting a theoretical escape, but now he thought better of it—there was no point in an exercise that would only depress him.

167

He could pass the time with thinking about Latisha instead, perhaps—with remembering the time they'd had together, and with speculating on what her real world must be like. Was there someone there she'd fashioned him in the likeness of? He'd heard of writers doing such things. But he preferred to think that if he was a figment of her imagination, he was at least an original one, and that whatever she'd felt for him hadn't been influenced by some other man somewhere.

He thought he could see movement in the clouds above the prison, something large—but that was ridiculous. No one flew over Caderousse; skydwellers avoided it like the plague, and respectable people wanted to keep it out of sight and mind.

. . . But there did seem to be a shadow hovering there a moment before passing away, and a small dark figure dropping out of the clouds towards the topmost layer of cells.

He had to be dreaming. That was the only way to explain why he was seeing someone who looked—from a distance, anyway—suspiciously like Latisha being let down into a high-security prison on purpose.

He scrambled to his feet anyway, crossing to the side of his cage nearest to the intruder, who was only a couple of levels away from him. Whoever it was had been quick and quiet enough so far that the patrolling guards hadn't caught on yet, and the prisoners certainly weren't going to raise any kind of alarm—at least those who were still capable of noticing she was there.

Then she dropped down a level, coming closer, and turned to scan the cells around her, bringing her face into clear view.

Rodrigo bit back a cry. It was Latisha.

It was her. She was here. She'd come back somehow, and she'd come to save him, something that would have been stupid from anyone else.

But she clearly knew this place like the back of her hand—she'd made it. Under other circumstances, Rodrigo might have been angry about that, but now that that knowledge was about to save his life, it seemed unfair to take offense.

Not to mention that he'd thought he'd never see her again and being handed a reunion after that had him feeling unusually forgiving.

He couldn't resist, and the sooner he got her attention, the better their chances would be anyway. It was too dangerous to shout, but he stamped one foot against the bars of the floor three times in rapid succession. His heavy boot raised a clanging that the guards should dismiss but that would hopefully—

She glanced down, and their eyes met through half a dozen layers of metal grids. To her credit, she didn't call out to him, but her eyes went wide, and she darted for the closest ladder, sliding down it without a thought and sprinting down the catwalk towards his cage.

The bars weren't spaced enough to get a finger through, let alone his hands to catch hold of her the way he wanted to, but when she pressed her hands flat against the door, he did the same on his side, just barely able to feel the warmth of her skin.

It was enough. She was here and real and they were going to be all right.

"Ellis," he breathed. Then, correcting himself, he said, "Latisha. You're here. You must have figured it out."

"Figured what out?" She looked like she might laugh or weep at any moment.

Rodrigo, for his part, just knew he was wearing a stupid-looking infatuated grin and didn't especially care.

"You said in your letter that you were leaving to make things right with this world. But if you'd just talked to me, I would have told you that was impossible. Nothing was ever going to be all right if you were gone."

Latisha choked out a laugh. "You are a hopeless romantic," she said, as if they didn't both know that already, "and also not actually wrong about things being impossible. It's a little more complicated than that." She ducked her head. "I'm so sorry," she

169

murmured. "For the heists, for this place existing for you to get thrown into . . . all of it. If there were a way to undo it, I would, but I can't."

"It's all right. I promise, it's all right. We'll have all the time in the world for you to explain, but just now, darling—"

Latisha's head snapped up at the endearment.

He suppressed a smirk at the confirmation that he could still surprise her considering she'd invented him. "Perhaps we should focus on getting out of here?"

There was a guard making his way towards them with clicking, unhurried, rhythmic stride, and two more coming from the other direction a bit further off.

Latisha glanced at them and, wonder of wonders, chuckled.

"I'll tell you a secret," she stage-whispered. "I wanted them to catch me."

The closest of the guards clapped a hand on her shoulder at that point, hauling her back from Rodrigo's cell. He was already reciting his recorded spiel. "You have been apprehended while trespassing in Caderousse Prison. Punishment for this crime is immediate and permanent imprisonment without trial. Do not resist." The automaton steered her towards the cell next door, the one with the skeleton. The index finger of his free hand was already folding back its shell of synthetic skin to expose the cylindrical key that would unlock any cell.

Rodrigo had about three seconds of panic and one and a half of realizing what Latisha was going to do.

Instead of resisting the guard's frog-marching like he clearly expected her to, she moved with him, causing him to turn too far and letting her steer him, with some effort, in a full turn until he was facing Rodrigo's cell again. This evidently disoriented him so much that she was able to grab hold of his arm and jab the exposed finger-key into the lock on Rodrigo's door, which swung open.

He scrambled out, and the automaton stumbled in, not recovering quite fast enough to prevent the door being slammed shut on him again.

Under the circumstances, Rodrigo really had no choice but to close the distance between himself and Latisha in a couple of quick strides and pull her in for a long, hard kiss—one that she almost immediately reciprocated. If he'd wondered at all whether she'd missed him as much as he missed her, the desperation with which she clung to him gave him all the answer he needed.

Then she pulled away, as the clanging sound of quite a lot more guards came closer. She tossed him a sword—the one he'd used in their sparring sessions if he wasn't mistaken.

He looked from it to her as she drew her own sword. "As glad as I am that you thought to bring me a weapon, I'm not sure how much good stabbing automaton guards will do," he commented. That was sort of the point of automaton prison guards, after all. They were nearly impossible to kill, and wounding them didn't stop them.

"We don't have to kill them," Latisha said, glancing back and forth at their possible escape routes. "We just have to keep them at bay and get through them."

"To the top level, right? For the *Rake* to pick us up," he hazarded.

"Nope," she tossed out with surprising confidence. "As far down as possible. I have a plan, trust me."

"Well, that's worked out well for me so far," he commented.

Latisha ducked her head slightly. "I said I was sorry."

"What? No, that wasn't sarcasm, I meant it."

Latisha actually gaped at that, but before she could recover, the guards were on them, and there was no time to do anything except fight.

It didn't take long to work out that this part of the plan chiefly relied upon him. Latisha was reasonably good with a sword—she ought to be, he'd trained her himself, and hadn't even gotten that distracted with flirting with her—but she was still relatively inexperienced.

The guards had the disadvantage of having been built to deal with unarmed, solitary prisoners, rather than two armed humans working together, but there were still a lot of them and not very much space to create distance.

They also, annoyingly, could learn, so Latisha's trick of getting one to open a cell and lock himself in only worked a few more times. That meant it was chiefly down to Rodrigo to clear a path, more by beating the guards back with sword strikes and the occasional elbowing and kicking than by doing any actual damage.

Latisha ended up back-to-back with him, keeping up a defense but mostly making sure they didn't get separated.

Somehow, they were able to work their way down three levels in this fashion, despite more and more guards crowding in on them. The other prisoners were cheering them on at this point, making more noise than they would have dared to without the guards being otherwise occupied.

Rodrigo briefly felt a twinge of guilt for not getting more people out, but it was already a miracle that he and Latisha were doing so well. If they managed this, they could pass the method on to other crews or maybe come back for some people.

Today, all he wanted was for the two of them to get out and get to safety . . . and maybe have some peace and a chance to ask and answer some questions before the next disaster struck.

Even that was starting to seem like too much to ask, however.

They were still only on the second level from the bottom, and hemmed in by what had to be every guard in the place. They could try to find a weak point in the ranks to push through, but it wasn't looking likely.

Except that, when he twisted around and caught a glimpse of Latisha's face, she was smiling.

Chapter 23

"I have a confession to make," Latisha said quietly.

"And what might that be, love?"

She resolutely ignored the shivers up her spine when he called her that; this was not the time. "I made this place for you to escape from." Latisha moved, despite the tight space, to stand facing Rodrigo, needing to see his face when she said this. "I never wanted you to do the seduction heists either. You were supposed to be a daring adventurer, and someday you were going to get locked in here and escape."

Rodrigo at least didn't look like he hated her yet; mostly he just looked confused.

She made herself go on, keeping half an eye on the steadily amassing guards in her peripheral vision. "I would've preferred to never bring that up, but I suppose it came in handy. Because as it turns out, the back door I built in is still here, even though I — you — never used it."

The catwalks weren't meant to hold this much weight at one time. She couldn't get an exact count, but she was willing to bet that every automaton guard in Caderousse was assembled on this level, blocking any escape route they might take. Even the ones that should have been off-shift in one of the gasbags must have been sent in.

She could almost feel the metal grating beneath her feet creaking with the weight. The metal of the structure was steel, but it was still vulnerable to corrosion, wear, and minor damage, and years of being suspended over the ocean without regular maintenance hadn't kept it in prime condition.

Keeping her eyes on Rodrigo's face to watch for some sign of distrust or alarm—relieved when she saw none—she sheathed her sword in one swift motion, leaned close, and whispered, "Do what I do."

Then she sprang back and, feeling slightly foolish, jumped in place. Rodrigo reacted quickly enough to imitate her motion at almost the same time, and their combined weight slamming into the same panel of overburdened catwalk caused it to give way from under them.

As she fell, Latisha had a brief, hilarious glimpse of the hole above them—ringed with startled, curious faces of a dozen guards—before she landed with a jolt on the bottom level, frantically remembering to bend her knees with the impact just in time.

Rodrigo had hit just a moment before her and steadied her as she stumbled. He glanced questioningly down the catwalk they'd landed on. It was a direct, clear path to one of the guard-storage gasbags, one that would now almost certainly be empty.

"You know," he remarked dryly, "they keep high-security prisoners on the upper levels because it's supposed to make it difficult for us to steal these things."

"They probably weren't counting on the prison's designer mounting a rescue," Latisha pointed out.

She had to fight not to grimace at the reference to her scrivening, but Rodrigo just laughed.

"I imagine not." He reached out and took her hand in his. "Shall we?"

They ran for it, and nothing came improbably popping up to stop them in the last hundred-yard sprint between them and freedom.

It was ridiculously easy to break into the gasbag and steal it. The guards that had rushed out to deal with them hadn't even bothered to shut the gondola door, let alone lock it.

Once they were inside, Latisha couldn't help but break down laughing at the sheer foolishness of it, even if it was foolishness that ended up helping them in their unlikely escape. Rodrigo was laughing too, but he caught her arm and hauled her along to find the bridge so they could complete their getaway—probably the wiser course of action. The guards were likely coming to try and break back in any moment now.

The bridge was easy to find and the takeoff easy to initiate, and they were buzzing away from Caderousse in mere minutes.

Everything about the escape itself had been relatively straightforward, Latisha reflected, at least for someone with her advantage.

The difficult part was going to be now, when they had to have a conversation about why she'd come back at all and what it meant.

"I assume you had a rendezvous point arranged with Linn beforehand?" Rodrigo inquired, fiddling with the navigational equipment.

She had. Latisha gave him the coordinates, then fell silent, trying to figure out what to say next.

"How you got her to agree to such a madcap scheme so quickly, I can't imagine. It usually takes me days to talk her around."

"We didn't necessarily have days, and everyone knew it." Saying it had her remembering all over again how Rodrigo had been, if briefly, in a place that most people equated with death. He was brushing it off so easily, but that was probably on her again, and all the perilous experiences she'd put him through, wasn't it?

That brought back the sick twist of guilt again. Even though she understood now that she couldn't just undo what she'd done, that didn't make the things she'd subjected people—specifically Rodrigo—to all right.

They needed to talk about this.

"I'm sorry," she blurted out before she could think better of it.

Rodrigo turned to look at her, one eyebrow raised in confusion. "For what? Breaking me out of a deadly and supposedly inescapable prison? I'm not sure what you feel the need to apologize for there."

Latisha threw up her hands. "For sticking you in a life where you just shrug off a brush with death like it was nothing. For making your crew think you're a feckless womanizer and sending you on fool's errands for years. And that's not even touching the larger societal problems that I can't undo without changing everything you and the rest of the crew are."

He wasn't supposed to look at her with so much affection when she said those things, or to cross to her and gently cup her shoulders in his strong, clever hands, but he did. "You didn't know," he said softly, "and when you did know, you stopped. All through the May Day heist, I kept thinking it at would happen any moment. I was waiting to not be in control anymore, but you let me be, once you knew I was real."

"And you ended up in jail," Latisha couldn't help but point out.

"I did. Getting arrested was the best moment of my life, because I knew you weren't pulling the strings. Well, the best moment until I saw you coming for me."

Latisha blushed and looked at the floor. "I didn't even know what had happened to you until a few hours ago, when I came back, and Linn told me. I just needed to be back here and see you again. If you hated me, I would've found somewhere else to go."

"Somewhere else in this world?" he clarified.

She nodded.

"But if you think there's so much wrong with it, why would you want to stay if you don't have to? I supposed the first time must have been an accident, with how disoriented you were."

Latisha looked up, startled, and saw that he was smirking with the knowledge of having made a telling logical point. "Because . . . " she sputtered, "because I love it. I made it to be the kind of world I would want to live in, and once I went back to where I came from, nothing seemed to fit anymore. And I . . . I want to be with you if you still want me."

Rodrigo made a thoughtful noise in the back of his throat. "So, you're saying your world isn't perfect and just?"

She snorted. "Far from it."

"Then why should this one be?"

Latisha opened her mouth, trying to formulate an argument, and found that she couldn't. Instead, she settled for a glare. "Stop derailing my attempts at penitence with logic."

"I will not." His hands slipped from her shoulders to pull her into an embrace. "I already forgave you for everything you did unknowingly, and that only left the time when you left without telling me. But now you're back, in rather spectacular fashion, so nothing needs to be forgiven."

She was sure she was supposed to still be tense with guilt and anxiety, but it was hard to stay like that when he held her like this. It was even harder to try and use logic when he started pressing kisses into her hair.

She let herself melt. "It can't just be this easy," she muttered stubbornly into his shirt.

"Whyever not?" he inquired, stepping back to examine her face.

"Because! Maybe you're fine with all of this right now when the adrenaline's going and you're still processing that I'm back and there aren't any complications yet, but eventually we'll fight, or you'll see something awful and remember I'm responsible and hate me for it, or it'll all just be too much and you'll be done with me. And —"

Rodrigo cut her off gently with a brief touch of his finger to her lips. "Or," he offered, "I'll keep getting arrested over and over now that we don't have a safety net, and you'll get fed up with breaking me out all the time. Or we'll run into some woman I stole from at some point, things will get messy, and you'll leave in a jealous rage. Or Floriane will find a way to come around and make trouble again—she's been arrested, but I can't see that lasting long

—and she'll try and shoot one or both of us. Who knows?" He spread his hands wide. "Alternatively, none of those things might happen, or if they do, we'll deal with them and work through them. I, for one . . . am willing to try."

If he kept saying things like that, he would be the death of her all on his own. "Well, so am I, or I wouldn't have come back." Which was true—she could talk all day long about how she'd missed the crew and the clothes and the smell of the air, but ultimately, she'd come back for the chance that he would still want her.

There was something else she really ought to say, but before she could, they burst through a cloud and she could see the *Rake*, hovering and waiting for them. "Look, we made it," she said instead, pointing. Then, after a moment's thought, "What are we going to tell the crew about where I was and why? Grammy knows—long story—and I could maybe lie to Asad and Ruby, but I think Linn saw me fall out of the sky."

Rodrigo slid an arm around her waist. "You could tell them part of the truth—that you can travel between worlds—and leave the scrivener part out. Although, how you would explain how you got us out of Caderousse in that case, I don't know."

"I don't know what they'll do if I tell them the whole truth," Latisha argued. "Isn't one existential crisis enough to be going on with?"

"Ah, but they would have you there to answer questions, unlike in my case," he pointed out. "I wouldn't worry too much. They know you. Whatever explanation you give, it won't change what they think of you too much."

She wasn't so sure about that. Perhaps she could postpone any explanations until she'd had a chance to talk it over with Grammy. They had a lot they needed to discuss anyway.

They were close enough now to leave the gasbag hovering in place and let Asad steer the *Rake* into position for them. Rodrigo locked the wheel and glanced around. "Sure you don't want to keep this one? There should be enough room for everyone on it, and they do say these are superior to skyships."

He was teasing; Latisha cracked a smile in response. "Nothing is superior to the *Rake* and we both know it." Slipping her hand into his as they started to leave the bridge, she took a deep breath. This needed to be said before she lost the moment. "Do you . . . love me, still?"

His answering look was incredulous, clearly not disbelieving that she would think he could do such a thing, as she'd feared, but disbelieving that she would have any doubt. "I never stopped."

"Well, I'm glad, because . . . I love you, too. And I think that's what let me come back."

They both moved in for the kiss at the same time. It wasn't a fairy-tale, credits-rolling kind of kiss—he still smelled of prison foulness and tasted like Lady Jennifer's champagne, and the adrenaline had worn off enough now for her to notice—but it felt undeniably real nonetheless, like coming home after far too long away.

The moment was cut off by the clanging of the *Rake*'s signal bell, and Rodrigo broke away muttering, "Clearly, someone is fed up with waiting for us."

But that was all right, and sort of its own homecoming, too.

They made their way back to the gondola door, and Asad had lined up the *Rake* so the deck was nearly level with them and only a short jump away. Once they'd leaped aboard, he had them soaring away almost immediately, no doubt eager to put as much distance between them, the stolen vehicle, and the prison as possible.

Latisha wasn't sorry to see the last of it herself, but she could barely spare any attention for it. Rodrigo had pulled her close against his side again, no doubt to present a united front to the crew—Asad was approaching from the helm now that their course was set, and everyone else was coming up from below. Linn, normally far from demonstrative, looked like she might want to hug them both. Ruby actually did, although she immediately backed away, looking embarrassed, while Asad, in a rare display of camaraderie, clapped Rodrigo on the shoulder as he welcomed him back.

Grammy, bringing up the rear, fixed Latisha with a look. "So, are you staying around this time?" The question, at face value, was probably something everyone was wondering, but the older woman's gaze made it clear that this was about a deeper issue — she was asking about what Latisha had done and decided in her time away, and whether the love that had brought her back was strong enough to hold her.

She looked around and glanced at Rodrigo, the man who had once been such an object of fear and loathing yet who had somehow come to hold her heart, and then nodded at Grammy.

"You couldn't get rid of me if you tried."

Epilogue

Grammy lay in her bunk in her cabin in the dark, and the voice that was not part of her thoughts spoke to her.

You see, it all worked out well in the end, Demodocus said, calm, untouchable, and matter-of-fact as ever.

"I know it did," she spoke into the darkness, barely whispering so as not to wake Ruby. "But I still don't see why we had to put them through that. Captain's heart was just about broken, and you had no way of knowing that she'd come back."

Her heart was here. She gave it to him before you spoke to her, and she would always have come back for it. But she had to know she had a choice to stay or go. She had to make the decision herself.

"You and your mind games make me sick sometimes. I wouldn't give it up—the seeing and the knowing—but I hated manipulating those two for no good reason."

On the contrary. I never do anything without a good reason. I've shown you what's coming. Both of them will be needed, and they must be absolutely sure of each other when the time comes. He had to know what she is, and she had to see him accept the truth. It was the only way.

"You're not even sorry."

Being sorry is not especially in my nature, not when the fate of so many worlds is at stake. But . . . I suppose I do regret, sometimes, what happens to the scriveners once they know. Once their eyes are opened, most of them stop writing, stop creating. It is a shame to see that talent cast aside.

"Doesn't stop you from doing it, though. Latisha won't be the last."

Unfortunately not.

"Who else are you going to inflict this misery on before this is all over?"

I can't always predict that, as you know. There are emergencies that sometimes fall outside of this particular plan. But there is one whom I've been meaning to have a word with for a while now. His world has so much potential . . . 'ancient green woods full of magic' is how you described it, I think.

Would you like to see?

Acknowledgments

Much like a well-executed heist, this book would have been impossible to do alone. Fortunately, I didn't have to. The following people were all instrumental along the way:

Cathy Ozog, Shannon Ozog Somes, and Gregory Roberts-Gassler, who were the initial test audience and instrumental in motivating me to actually finish the story, listening to many Scrivenersverse ramblings along the way.

Gabi Cardenas, Maddie Clemons, Nathalie Knowles, Shannon Ozog Somes, and Gregory Roberts-Gassler, my inestimable beta readers who provided unique insights that made the Rakeworld so much better and more richly detailed.

Jamie Noble Frier, who contributed the cover art and design, bringing Latisha and Rodrigo to life and surpassing all expectations.

Chelsea Beam, who brought amazing editing to the table, trimming the sails of my run-ons and taking this story to incredible heights.

Special thanks goes out to my family—my mom for passing her love of stories on to me, my dad for believing I could be a writer before I was even sure about it, and my siblings and grandparents for always asking what I was writing and listening to my rants.

Lastly, none of this would have been possible without the grace of God, who blessed me with all of these wonderful individuals and preserved my sanity through the process of bringing this story to fruition.

About the Author

Chloe Taton has always wanted to visit another, more fantastical world. She has not yet succeeded, but until then, she makes do with stories in almost any form, especially the printed word. Someday, she will get around to writing all the stories clamoring for attention in her brain, in between bouts of obsessively detailed cosplay and praying for more stratus clouds and fewer sunny days. She lives in Everett, WA, but can be most easily found at chloetatonwrites.com.